THE USBORNE BOOK OF CUTAWAY BOATS

Christopher Maynard

Designed by
Isaac Quaye & Steve Page

Illustrated by: Mick Gillah, Sean Wilkinson, Ian Cleaver, Gary Bines, Justine Peek and artists from the School of Illustration, Bournemouth and Poole College of Art and Design.

Consultants: Guy Robbins & David Topliss, National Maritime Museum, London

Edited by Jane Chisholm

Additional designs by Robert Walster

Usborne Publishing wish to thank the following for their help with this book:

Joan Barrett, Atlantic Container Line · Alan L. Bates · Historic Royal Dockyard, Chatham · Michael Leek, Cordwainer's College · Flarecraft Inc. · Howard Smith (London) Ltd · Incat Designs Ltd., Japan Ship Centre · National Motorboat Museum · O.Y. Nautor Ab. · P & O · P & O European Ferries · Princess Cruises · Royal National Lifeboat Institution · Eamon Holland, Strategic Advertising · Vasa Museum, Stockholm · Yamaha Motor (UK) Ltd. · Yanmar Diesel Engine Co., Ltd.

Contents

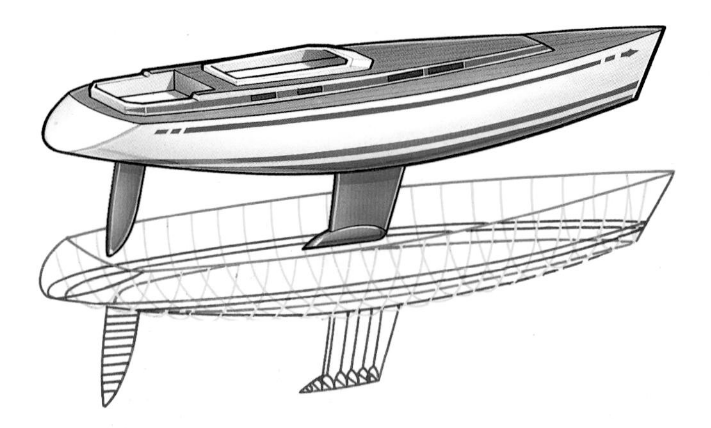

Words in *italic* type

Words which appear in *italic* type and are followed by a small star (for example, *knots**) can be found in the glossary on page 31.

Introduction

Boats have been around since Stone Age times. The earliest boats - dugout canoes, log rafts and frames of sticks covered in animal skins - were all paddled or rowed.

The Ancient Egyptians, in around 3000BC, were the first to use sails to harness the wind. By doing so, they discovered a much easier way to travel, and created enough power to drive much bigger boats.

But really large ships need engines to power them, and it's only in the past 200 years that these have come into use. Some run on diesel, but the fastest and biggest ships use gas or steam turbines.

A tug boat

This is an old tug that was used about 70 years ago to tow ocean-going ships in and out of port. Its power came from a large steam engine that ran on coal.

How boats float.

When a boat is placed in water, it pushes water aside, or displaces it. The water pushes back with a force called upthrust. The size of the upthrust depends on the weight of water displaced. In order to float, an object must displace enough water so that the upthrust is as great as the weight of that object.

The amount of water an object displaces depends on its shape. For example, a ball of clay will sink, but if you hollow it out into a bowl shape it will float. By changing the clay's shape, you have increased the amount of water it displaces. This is what boat builders do. A solid lump of steel would sink, but a ship made of hollowed out steel will float.

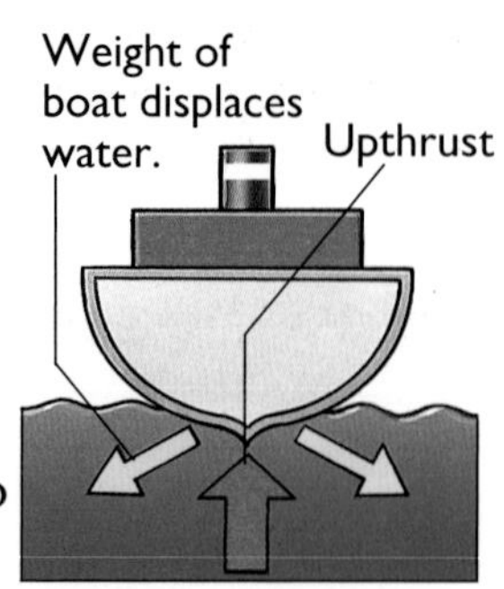

How boats steer

A boat is steered by a rudder or a steering oar, which is a big blade-shaped object at the stern (the back of the boat). This cuts into the flow of water and can swivel to deflect the water to either side. As the water pushes hard against the blade, it causes the stern to swing around, pointing the bow of the boat in a new direction.

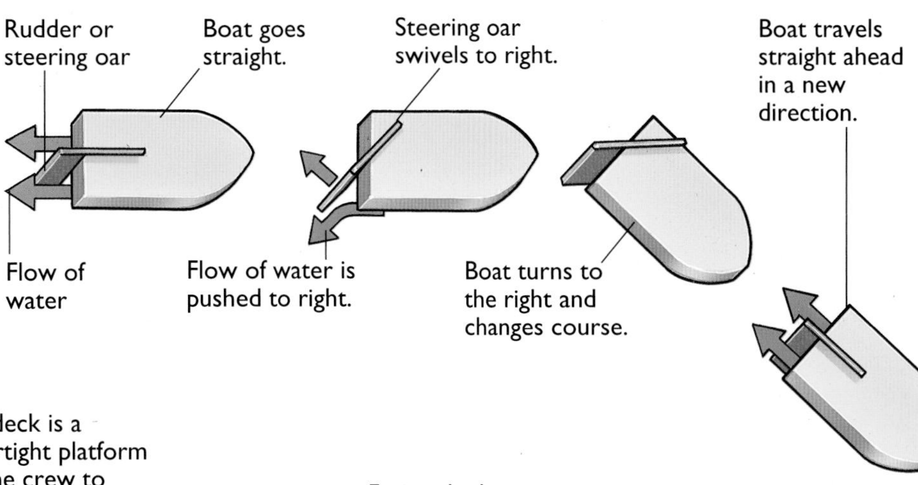

The funnel lets out smoke from the burning coal.

The deck is a watertight platform for the crew to work on.

Facing the bow, the left is called the port side, the right is the starboard side.

The back of a ship is called the stern. It is rounded to let the boat slip easily through the water.

The body of a boat is called the hull. This one is made of tough, watertight steel.

This is the hold, where freight is stored and the engine and fuel are kept.

Coal fires heat water in the boilers, making steam. This drives the engine, providing the power to turn the propeller.

This is the propeller. As it spins, it drives the ship forward.

This is the rudder, which steers the boat.

How boats sail

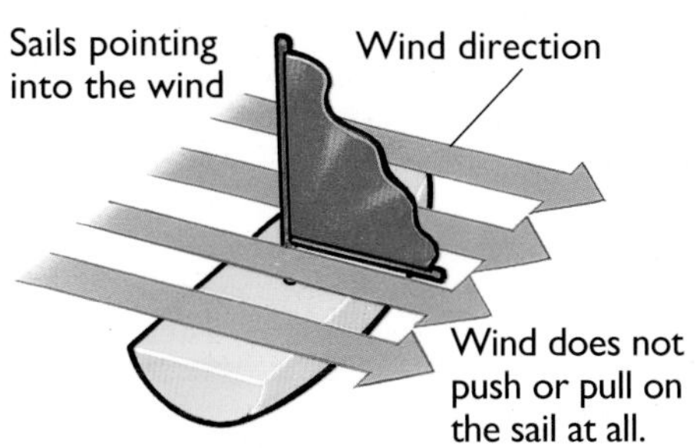

Sails sideways to the wind

Wind creates lift at the front of the sail and pulls the boat forward.

Wind pushes on back of sail and shoves boat along.

Sails too far into the wind

No pull on front of sail

Wind still pushes against sail.

A boat moves by trapping the wind in its sails. But if the sails point directly into the wind, they only flap noisily, producing no power.

Sideways to the wind, the sail fills and creates two forces: lift, which pulls the boat forward, and push, which shoves the boat along.

But if a sail is hauled too far into the wind, the airflow behind it breaks up and stops pulling. The sail loses lift and produces much less power.

Triremes

About 2,500 years ago, in Ancient Greece, the most powerful and famous warship in the world was the trireme. It was big, fast and deadly, even though it was always rowed into battle.

As Greek cities grew rich and powerful, fleets of triremes were built to patrol the waters of the eastern Mediterranean. These ships cost a great deal to run, so only the richest cities, such as Athens or Corinth, could afford very many of them.

The main mast and the foremast each had one sail. The sails were only used on longer journeys when the wind was in the right direction.

Olympias

In 1985, a group of ship lovers and historians from all over the world launched a full-size replica trireme. It was called *Olympias* and, fittingly, it was built in Greece.

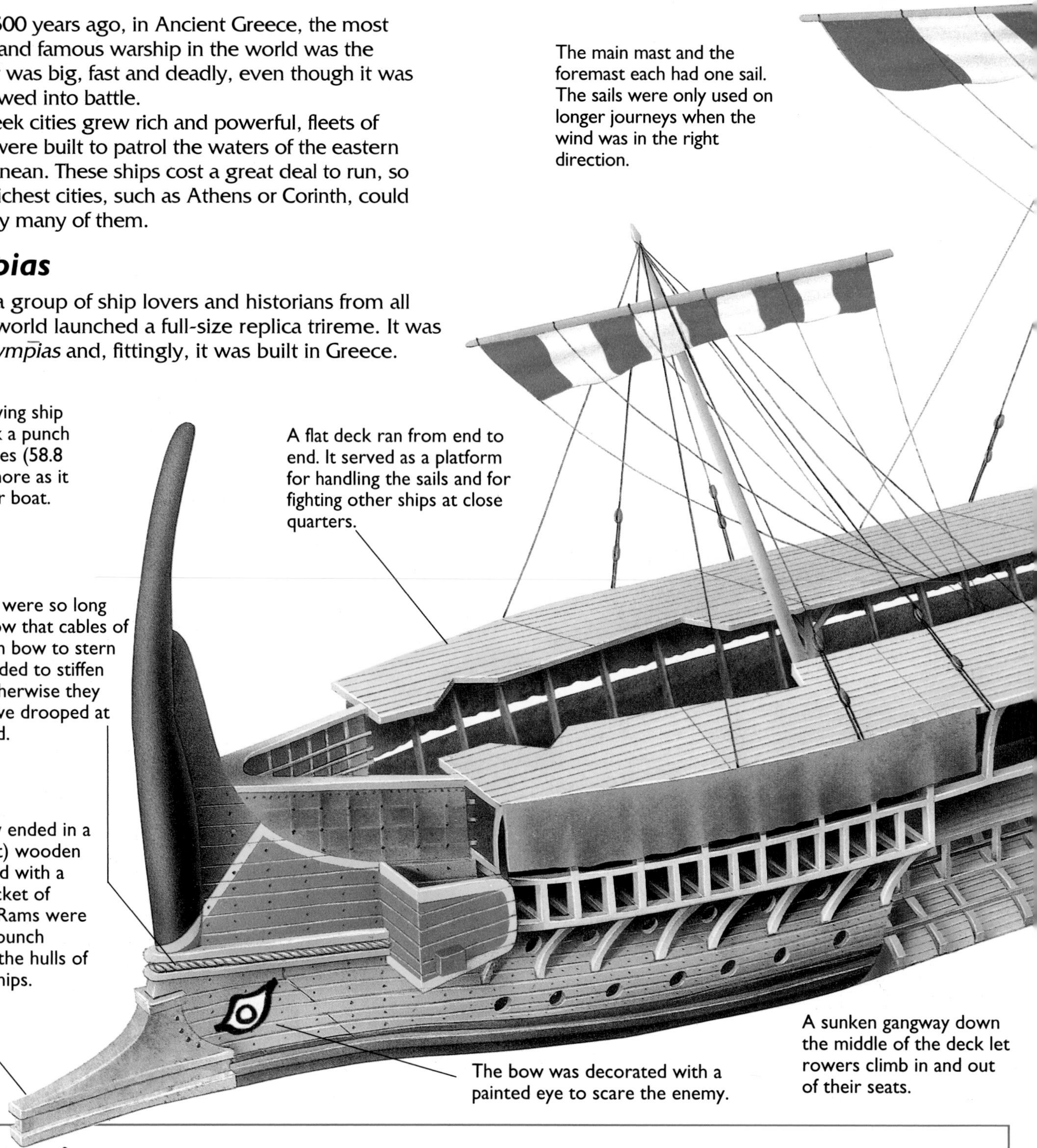

A fast-moving ship might pack a punch of 60 tonnes (58.8 tons) or more as it hit another boat.

A flat deck ran from end to end. It served as a platform for handling the sails and for fighting other ships at close quarters.

Triremes were so long and narrow that cables of rope from bow to stern were needed to stiffen them. Otherwise they would have drooped at either end.

The bow ended in a 2m (6.5ft) wooden ram fitted with a heavy jacket of bronze. Rams were used to punch holes in the hulls of enemy ships.

The bow was decorated with a painted eye to scare the enemy.

A sunken gangway down the middle of the deck let rowers climb in and out of their seats.

The engine room

Three banks of rowers were the engine that drove a trireme. They all used incredibly long oars, and could drive a ship at an amazing speed of over eight *knots** (almost 15 km or 9 miles an hour) all day long. This was much faster than it could travel by sail. When going a long distance in a hurry, triremes were almost always rowed. A long day's voyage from dawn to dusk might cover as much as 220km (136 miles).

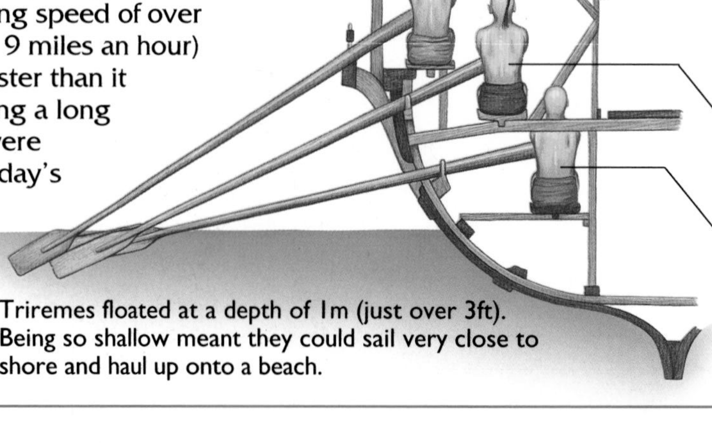

The upper rowers were called thranites. They sat in two rows of 31.

Middle rowers were called zygites. They sat in two rows of 27.

On the bottom tier were the thalamites. They sat in rows of 27, too.

Triremes floated at a depth of 1m (just over 3ft). Being so shallow meant they could sail very close to shore and haul up onto a beach.

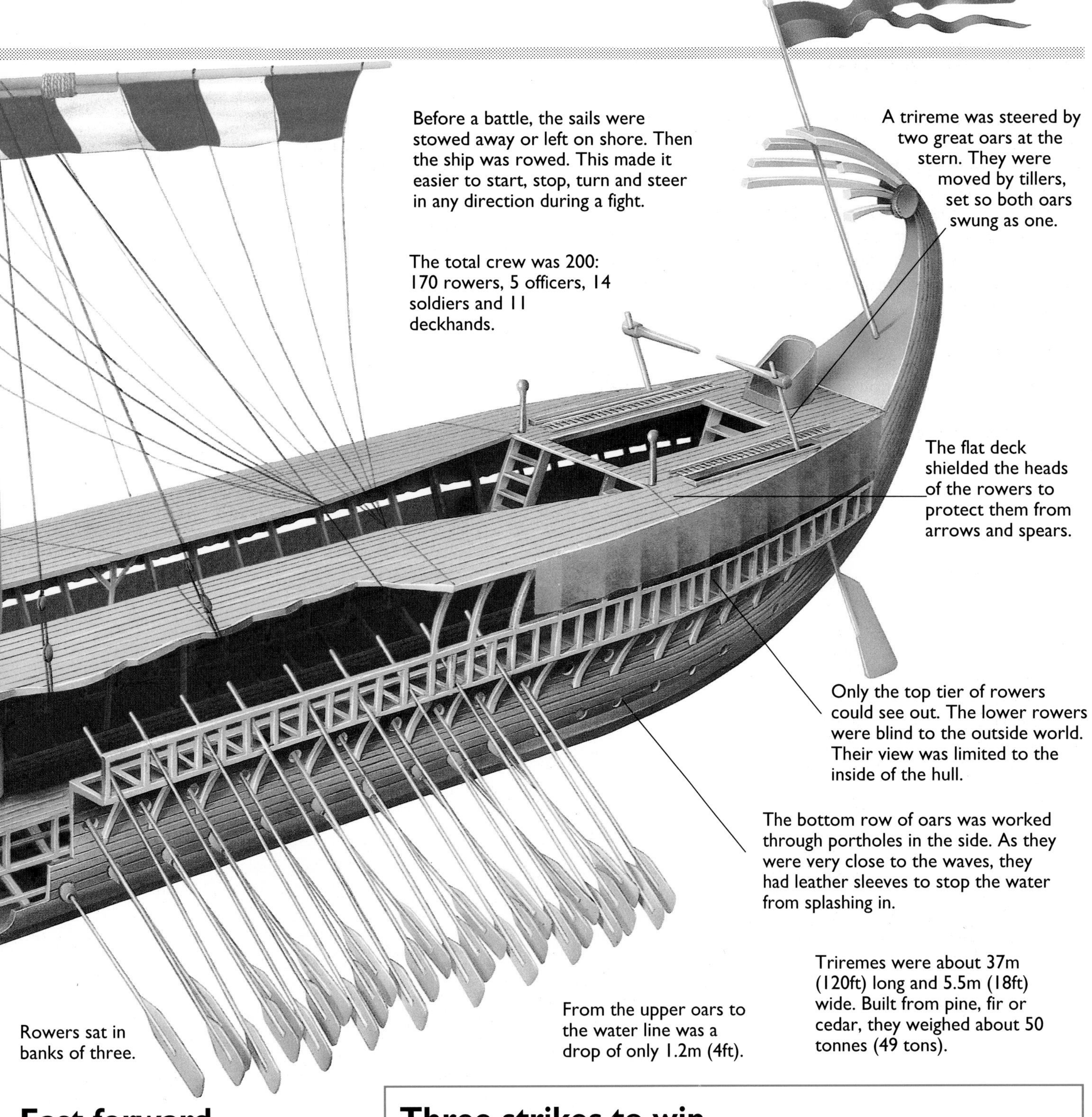

Fast forward

Trireme oars were long - 4.3m (14ft) from tip to handle. That's far higher than the ceiling of most modern rooms. The Ancient Greeks knew that the blade of a long oar swept much farther - and more powerfully - through the water than a short oar.

A Greek rower making a single stroke of his oar.

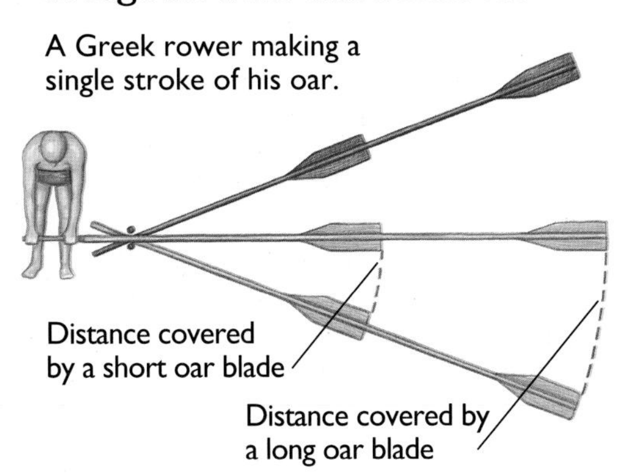

Three strikes to win

At the start of battle, triremes often faced off in two long lines. Each ship would pick out a target, then dart forward to try to ram an opponent and sink him. The best places to aim for were the stern and sides of another ship.

A trick often used was to sweep around the far end of the opposing line of ships and strike from the rear.

Sometimes a ship made for a gap in the line, then veered at the last moment to smash into the side of an enemy with its ram and shear off its oars.

A daring move was to break through a gap in the line, wheel and strike from behind.

The Age of Sail

Rowing is fine for lightweight boats, but it takes a lot more power to drive a really big ship through the water. For thousands of years, people relied on the wind. Using masts and sails, they were able to harness its energy to propel big ships all over the world.

The Vasa

The *Vasa*, launched in 1628, was the pride of the Swedish navy. But, because of a faulty design, she sailed a very short distance before sinking. Raised from the sea in 1961, she is the only complete 17th century warship in the world.

The Vasa	
Length:	69m (226ft)
Width:	12m (39ft)
Height:	53m (174ft)
Weight:	1,300 tonnes (1,274tons)
Guns:	64 guns
Crew:	135 sailors 300 soldiers

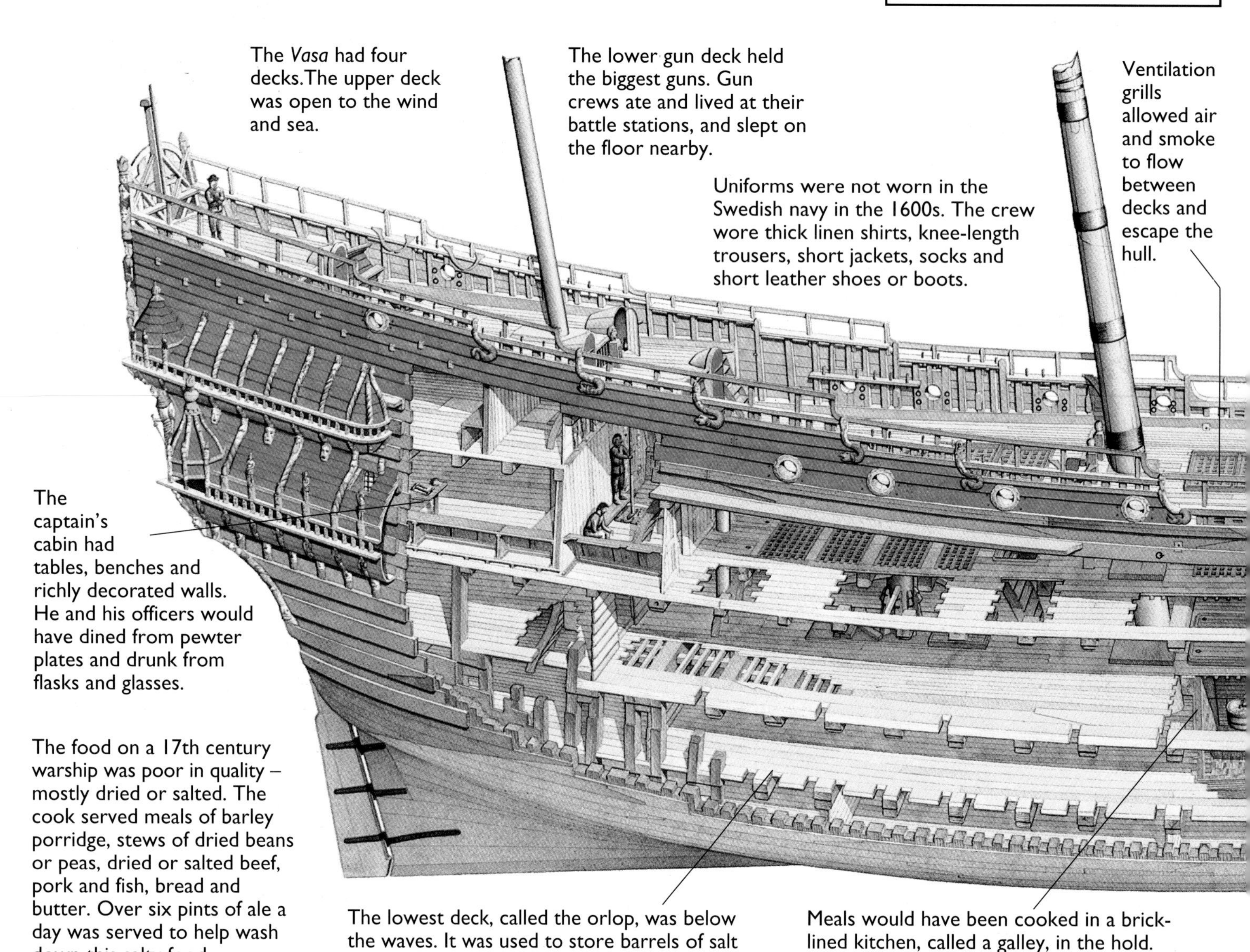

The *Vasa* had four decks.The upper deck was open to the wind and sea.

The lower gun deck held the biggest guns. Gun crews ate and lived at their battle stations, and slept on the floor nearby.

Ventilation grills allowed air and smoke to flow between decks and escape the hull.

Uniforms were not worn in the Swedish navy in the 1600s. The crew wore thick linen shirts, knee-length trousers, short jackets, socks and short leather shoes or boots.

The captain's cabin had tables, benches and richly decorated walls. He and his officers would have dined from pewter plates and drunk from flasks and glasses.

The food on a 17th century warship was poor in quality – mostly dried or salted. The cook served meals of barley porridge, stews of dried beans or peas, dried or salted beef, pork and fish, bread and butter. Over six pints of ale a day was served to help wash down this salty food.

The lowest deck, called the orlop, was below the waves. It was used to store barrels of salt beef and pork and other dried food. Sails, ropes and spare equipment was kept here too.

Meals would have been cooked in a brick-lined kitchen, called a galley, in the hold. A cauldron hung over an open fire. Smoke flowed freely up to the decks above.

Packing a big punch

Vasa was one of the most powerful ships of the Swedish Navy. It carried 64 guns, including 48 big ones able to fire 11kg (24 lb) cannonballs. Together they weighed over 72 tonnes (71 tons).

The *Vasa*'s guns were the most high-tech weapons of their time. But they were slow. Ten rounds an hour was considered outstanding. Between each firing, the gun had to be cleaned and left to cool.

Cannon is loaded with a charge and cannonball.

Cannon is pulled through gunport and aimed.

Firing hole is cleaned and small hole made in main charge.

Gunpowder is poured into firing hole.

Gunpowder is lit with an explosive fuse.

Vasa Museum

Rigged for sailing

The *Vasa* was a three-masted ship. She could put up ten sails in all, and a flutter of pennants and flags. At the time of sinking she was flying four sails. The other six were still in lockers. Today they are preserved intact in the Vasa Museum in Stockholm.

Royal warship

The *Vasa* was a fighting ship, but she was also built to show off the wealth and power of the King of Sweden, Gustavus Adolphus. From top to bottom, the entire stern was richly carved with hundreds of gilded figures and ornaments, including a huge royal coat of arms flanked by two crowned lions. Even the hatch covers of the gunports had faces of roaring lions carved onto them.

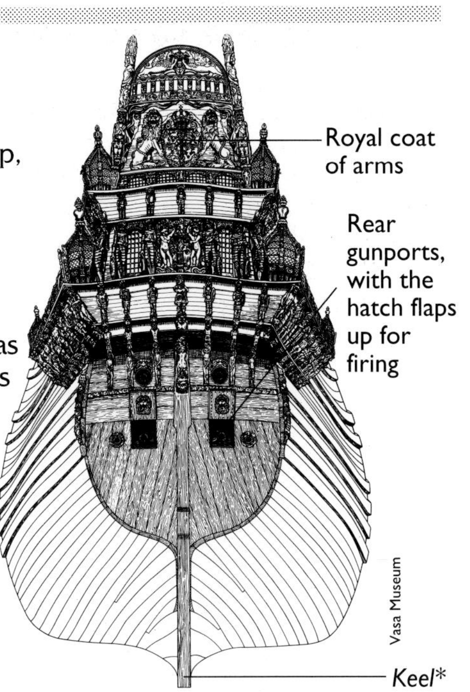

Vasa Museum

Over 1,000 oak trees were cut down to build the ship.

Grinning lion heads were carved onto the insides of the gun hatches. They would have been revealed to the enemy only when the hatches flipped up and the guns became visible.

The cannons poked out through holes in the hull called gunports. These were covered by wooden hatches, hung outside, that were lifted by ropes when the guns were ready to fire.

120 tonnes (118 tons) of stone *ballast** were packed in the hold to balance the weight of the masts and sails.

Gunpowder was stored in the hold, well below the water line.

The gun decks were dark, damp and crowded. The ship had no heating to keep out the chill.

Why did the *Vasa* sink ?

The *Vasa* sank because she was top-heavy. She was built too big and strong, and had too many heavy guns on the deck for the size of *hull**. She was also far too narrow to carry all that weight above the water line and still keep her balance. Just a mild gust of wind was enough to overturn her.

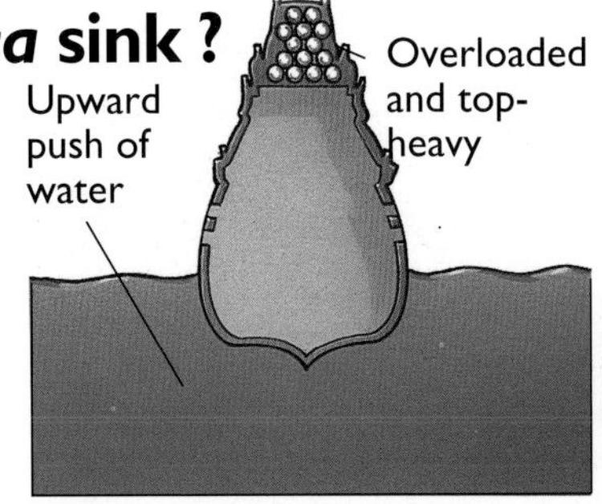

Although the *Vasa* was heavy, she could still float, because the upward push of water was equal to her weight. But being top-heavy made her unstable.

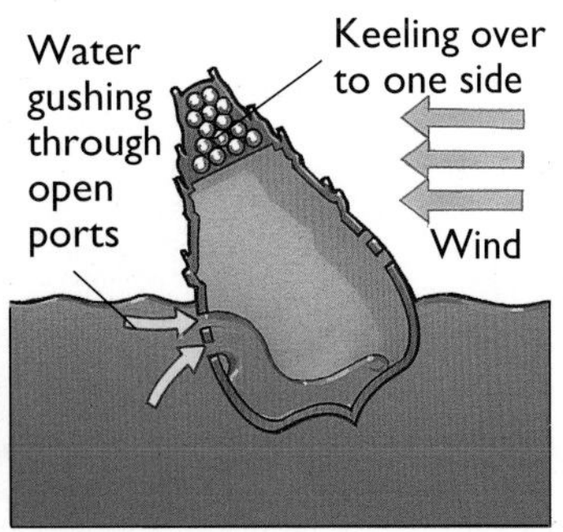

The ship began to roll heavily in the breeze and a sudden gust of wind made her lean sharply to one side. Then water began to flood in through open gunports.

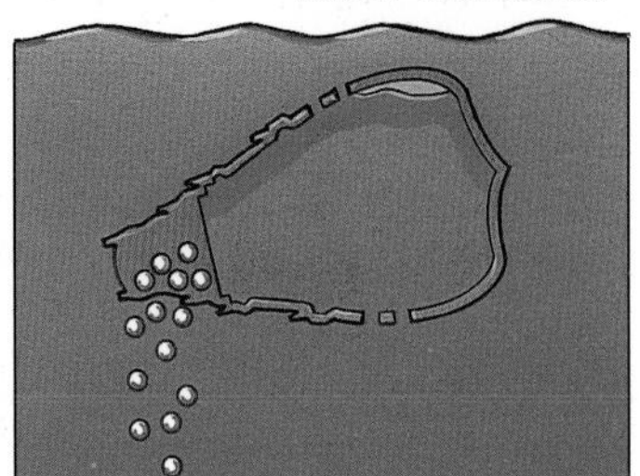

The water flooding in added extra weight to the ship, overcoming the upward push of the water below. The ship sank like a stone.

Steamships

In the 1800s, steam engines began to be installed in ships powered by sail, like *H.M.S.Gannet* shown here. This new source of power enabled a ship to travel without being dependent on winds or tides. With an engine to drive a propeller, it could make headway even in complete calm.

Historic Dockyard, Chatham

***H.M.S.Gannet* was a three-masted ship built by the British Navy to protect the sea routes of the empire.**

The ship had a crew of 140 men and boys.

Foredeck

H.M.S. Gannet was fitted with six medium guns that fired shells of solid steel, and six to eight machine guns.

At full speed, the engine could drive the ship at 11.5 knots. Yet under sail the ship went even faster - sometimes as much as 15 knots.

Every corner of the hold was stuffed with equipment intended to last for two or three years. Spare parts for the ship were almost impossible to find in the regions to which she sailed.

The *Gannet* carried over 142 tonnes (140 tons) of coal in her bunkers, enough to travel more than 1,600km (994 miles).

Ten iron bulkheads (walls with watertight doors) divided up the hull. They prevented the whole hull from flooding if any part of it was holed.

The hull was built as an iron frame. A double layer of thick teak planks was bolted onto it.

Switching to sail

When the *Gannet* wanted to sail, the engine was shut down. The funnel - which lowered like a telescope - was dropped and the sails were hoisted.

As the propeller (also known as the screw) now slowed the ship down, it was unhooked and lifted out of the water. The crew used a big deck winch and chain to raise it.

Steam engines

Steam ships are powered by engines which have boilers and furnaces to produce steam. Once the steam is at high pressure, it is piped to a small cylinder. It then flows on to a large cylinder at lower pressure. These two cylinders drive the pistons that turn the propeller that drives the ship forward.

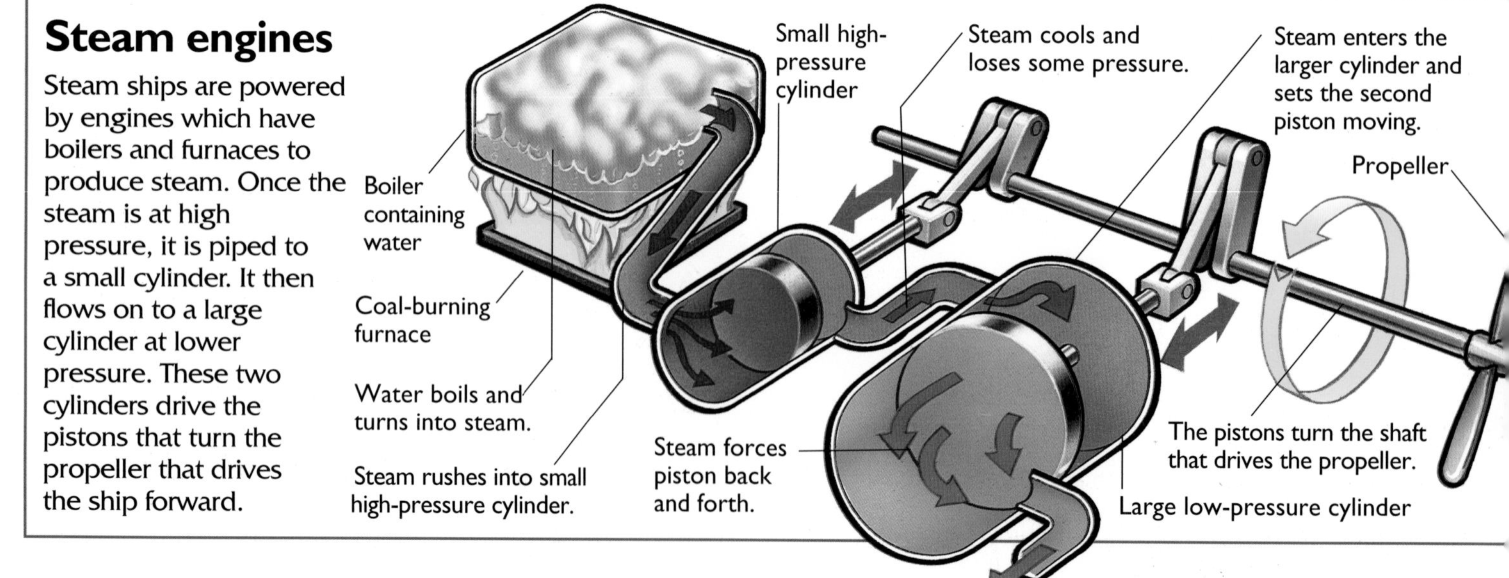

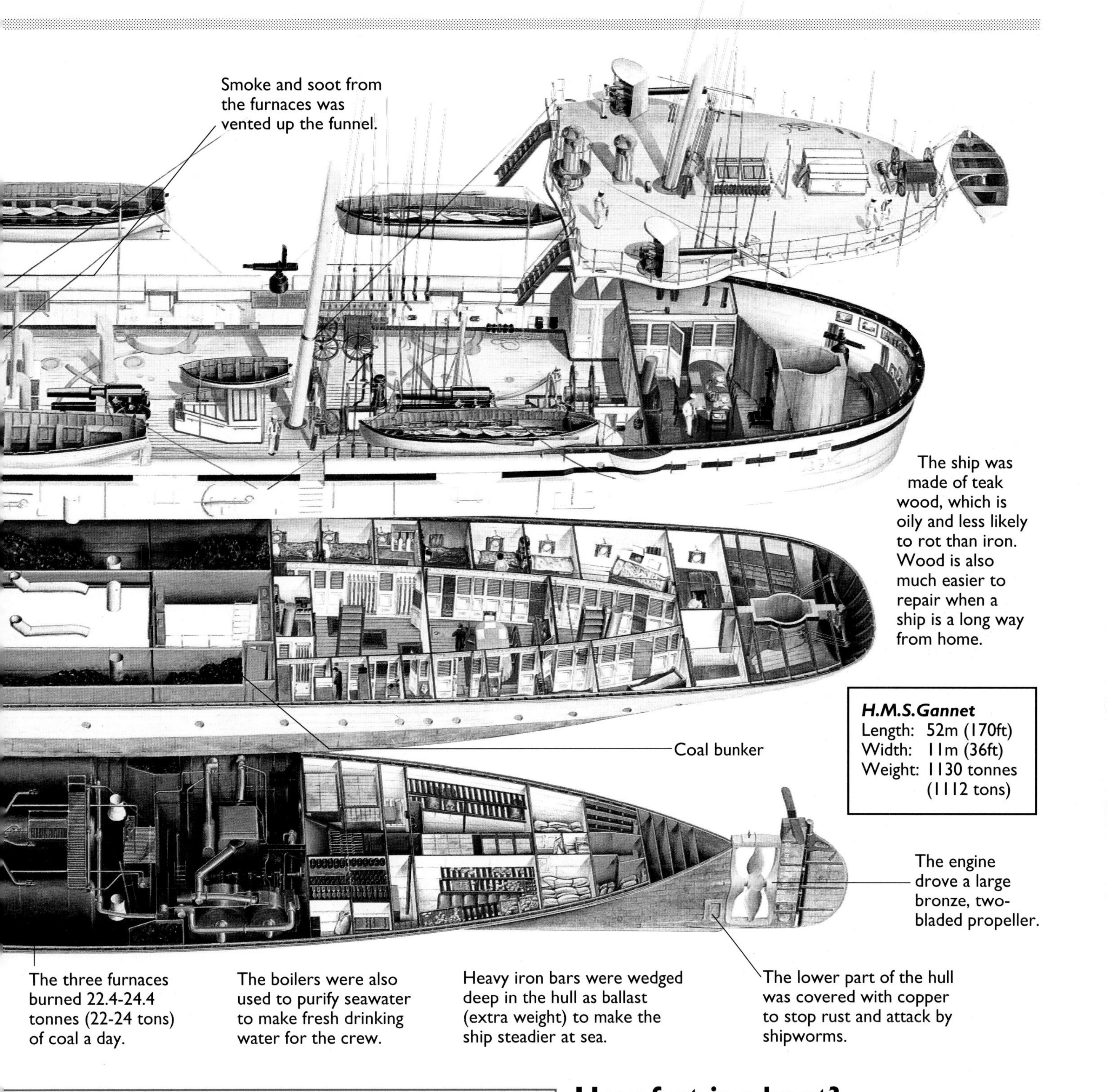

***H.M.S.Gannet's* engine and propeller**

Weight:	45 tonnes (44.3 tons)	Steam:	27kg (60lbs)
Length:	4.8m (15ft)	Power:	1100 *horsepower**
Cylinders:	2	Propeller width:	4m (13ft)
Boilers:	3	Propeller weight:	16 tonnes (15.7 tons)
		Propeller speed:	100 revolutions (turns)per minute

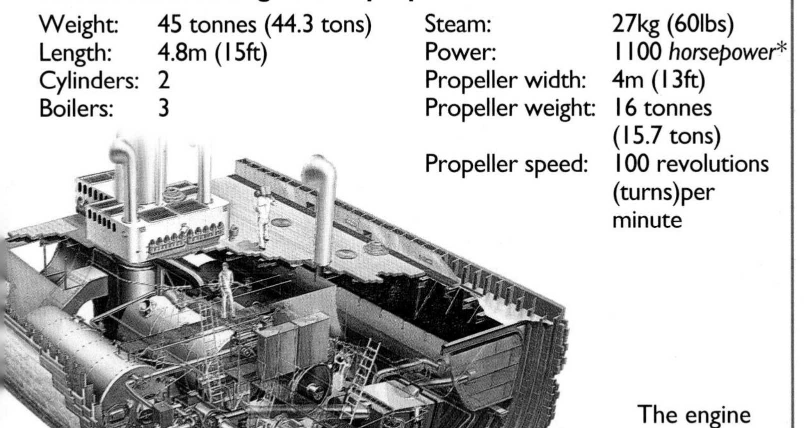

How fast is a knot?

A ship's speed is measured in knots. One knot is the same as 1.8km/h (just over a mile an hour). The word comes from the old custom of throwing a knotted rope, tied to a small plank, over the bow. As the wood floated toward the stern, knots in the rope were counted out to calculate the ship's speed.

Riverboats

The riverboat fleet that plied the Mississippi River basin in the 1800s was everything that trucks, trains and planes are today. For years it was the main form of transportation in the region. In 1860, a total of 10 million tons of cargo was shipped this way.

Riverboats that carried passengers and freight were called packets. The biggest were stately palaces that ran long distance express services. They were lightly built, flimsy even, compared to ocean-going ships. They had flat, shallow hulls, since anything deeper than 1.5m (5ft) really limited the places they could get to. But they all had huge steam engines to battle upstream against fast-flowing currents.

The Rob't. E. Lee

The *Rob't. E. Lee*, named after the Confederate commander-in-chief of the southern troops in the American Civil War, was the most celebrated riverboat of all. Built in Indiana in 1866, for the next ten years she worked the Mississippi up and down from New Orleans.

The Rob't. E. Lee

Length:	87m (285ft)
Width:	14m (46ft)
Engines:	2 steam engines
Boilers:	8 boilers producing 55kg (120lbs) of steam each
Weight:	1,432 tonnes (1,456 tons)
Fuel:	Coal and wood burning

Smoke from the boiler was discharged from two smokestacks, which towered high above the pilothouse. This meant the sparks could burn out before they drifted down to the decks.

Three fire pumps and long reels of hose were carried in case of fire.

The captain ran the ship from the pilothouse.

Boiler

The main cabin was furnished with everything from a velvet carpet to rosewood chairs and sofas.

The entire ship was built of wood, nails, bolts and iron fastenings.

The main deck was used entirely for cargo.

Two steam engines generated 2,700*hp** of power, enough to drive her along at over 32 kmph (20mph) in calm waters.

Main deck

Deck cargo

Riverboats took passengers and baggage, but their main business was freight, especially cotton. They carried it from all over the southern states of the USA down to New Orleans to be shipped overseas.

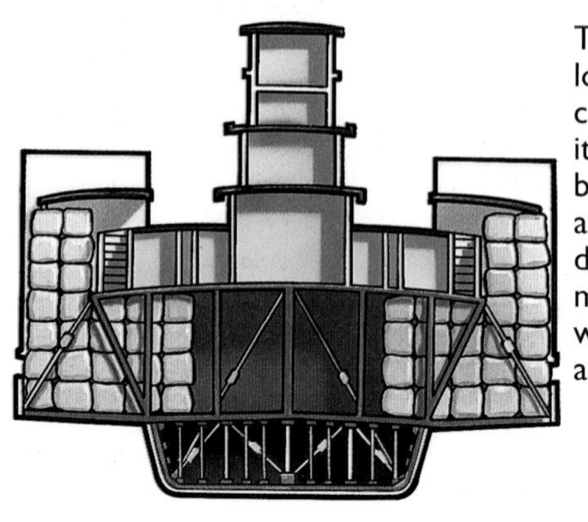

The *Rob't. E. Lee* once loaded 5,741 bales of cotton along the sides of its main deck.They could be stacked one on top of another, past all three decks. Passengers might make a whole trip without ever glimpsing any scenery.

Paddlewheels

Riverboats were powered by huge paddlewheels, mounted on each side, or at the stern. The big advantage over propellers was that they didn't dip below the hull, so the boats could keep going in very shallow waters.

At the end of the arms, wide planks of wood were bolted on to make the paddles.

The wheel was turned by a heavy central shaft linked to the engine.

The arms were braced to stop them flexing as the wheel turned.

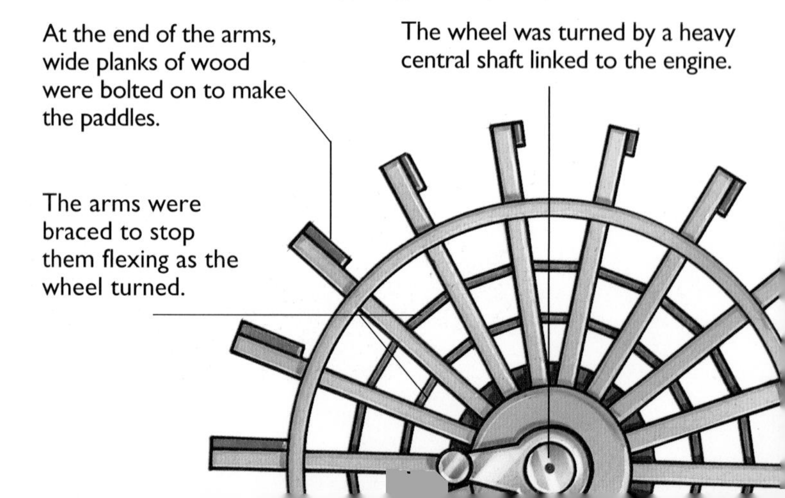

Side-wheelers and stern-wheelers

All riverboats had flat, shallow hulls, no keel and did not float very deep in the water.

Side-wheelers had one paddlewheel on each side, and an overhanging main deck which stuck out far beyond the hull. Stern-wheelers had only one wheel at the back, and their main deck was a lot narrower.

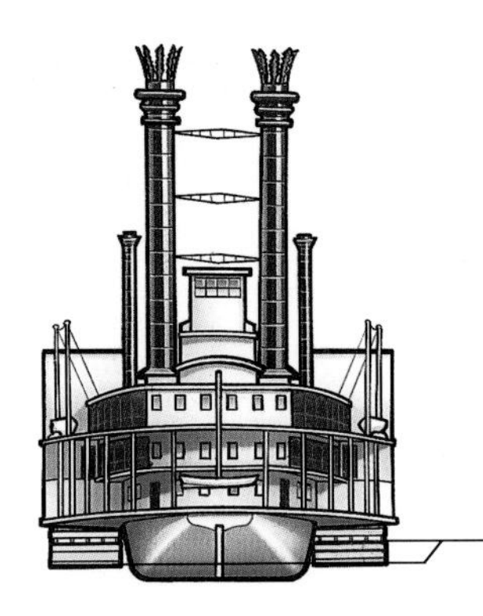

Side-wheeler seen from the bow (front)

Paddlewheels did not dip below the bottom of the hull. This protected them from rocks, logs and other clutter lying on the bed of the river.

Stern-wheeler seen from the stern (back)

Braces and chains

The hulls of riverboats were so long and thin that they became rather floppy. The bow and stern tended to sag into the water, a habit known as hogging. To correct this, sets of posts and chains were rigged up on deck to stiffen the frame of the hull.

Wooden posts

Hog chains

From bow to stern, sets of hog chains were rigged above the deck to stiffen the hull. They were made of lengths of iron rod, screwed together and braced by wooden posts.

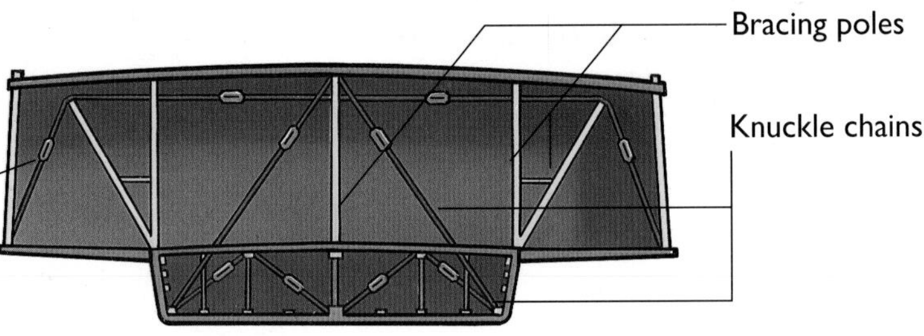

Cross-section of hull showing chains from side to side

The Great Race

In 1870, the *Rob't. E. Lee* gained lasting fame for itself in a great river race against the *Natchez*.

Both boats were due to leave New Orleans at 5pm on June 30th, bound for St. Louis, and the event grew into a feverishly-awaited race. Hundreds of thousands of dollars were laid as bets, and a huge, excited crowd lined the riverbanks to see the start.

The *Rob't. E. Lee* pulled away a couple of minutes before 5pm, her rival four minutes later. Throughout the lengthy race she was never really challenged again, although a leak in one of her boilers almost put out the fires below before it was finally plugged. The loss of speed let the *Natchez* get within 400 yards for a short while. On the last stage, by chance, night fog let the *Robt. E. Lee* gain several hours lead. She finally arrived in St. Louis on July 4th, a record 3 days, 18 hours and 14 minutes after setting out (and more than 6.5 hours ahead of the *Natchez*). To this day, no steamboat has ever beaten her time.

St. Louis (Finish line)

Cairo

Memphis

Vicksburg

Mississippi River

Natchez

New Orleans (Start of race)

Yachts

Using sail power today may seem old-fashioned, but modern yachts are very different from their forerunners. Their hulls are made from synthetic materials and super-strong glue, which is far tougher and longer-lasting than wood. The masts are shaped from lightweight metal, which is lighter than wood and doesn't rot in salt water. Many yachts are equipped with quiet diesel engines, as well as the latest satellite navigation gear, two-way radios and depth finders.

The *Swan 55*

The *Swan 55* is a single-masted yacht, known as a sloop. This yacht is built beside the Baltic Sea, in northern Finland, and is designed to be sailed across oceans. It has a deep, rounded hull and high sides. These features are common to all cruising yachts, making them stable and dry at sea.

Modern sails are made of terylene, a strong material which holds its shape well.

Navigation ar

The helmsman steers the yacht from the cockpit.

Small sundeck

The rear deck locker stores gas bottles for the stove, a life raft and ropes.

The rudder steers the yacht. It is moved by wires linked to a wheel in the cockpit. The rudder's long blade digs deep into the water to keep the boat dead on course.

Fully-equipped galley (kitchen)

Locker space between the inside walls and the hull

The three-blade propeller is driven by a six-cylinder, 116*hp** diesel engine. In calm waters it can do 10 *knots**.

There is a sound-proofed walk-in engine room.

The *Swan 55*	
Length:	16.7m (55ft)
Width:	4.8m (16ft)
Weight:	23 tonnes (22.5 tons)
Draught:	2.6m (8ft)
Sail area:	125m^2 (1345ft^2)

Different yacht types

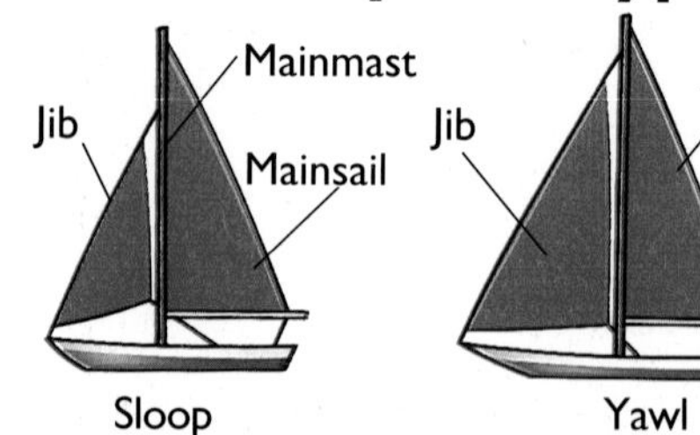

Sloop

Jib

Mainsail

Mizzenmast

Mizzensail

Yawl

Jib

Mainsail

Mizzenmast

Mizzensail

Ketch

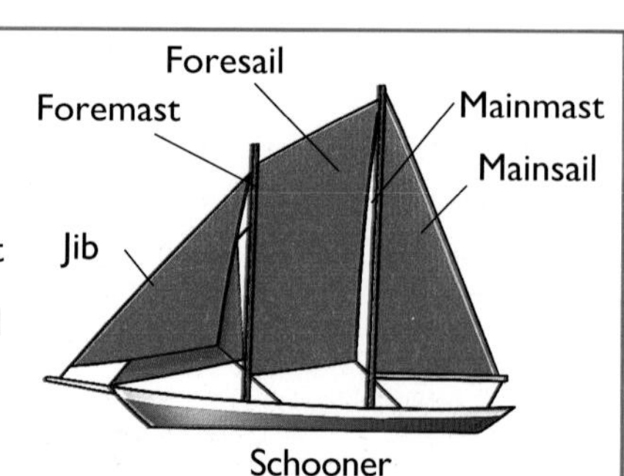

Schooner

Sailing yachts get their names from the way their masts and sails are rigged. A boat rigged with one mast is known as a sloop.

Yawls and ketches have two masts and can fly three or more sails. A mainsail, mizzensail and jib are the most common.

Schooners have a foremast ahead of the mainmast. They are bigger and can carry more sails than most other kinds of yachts.

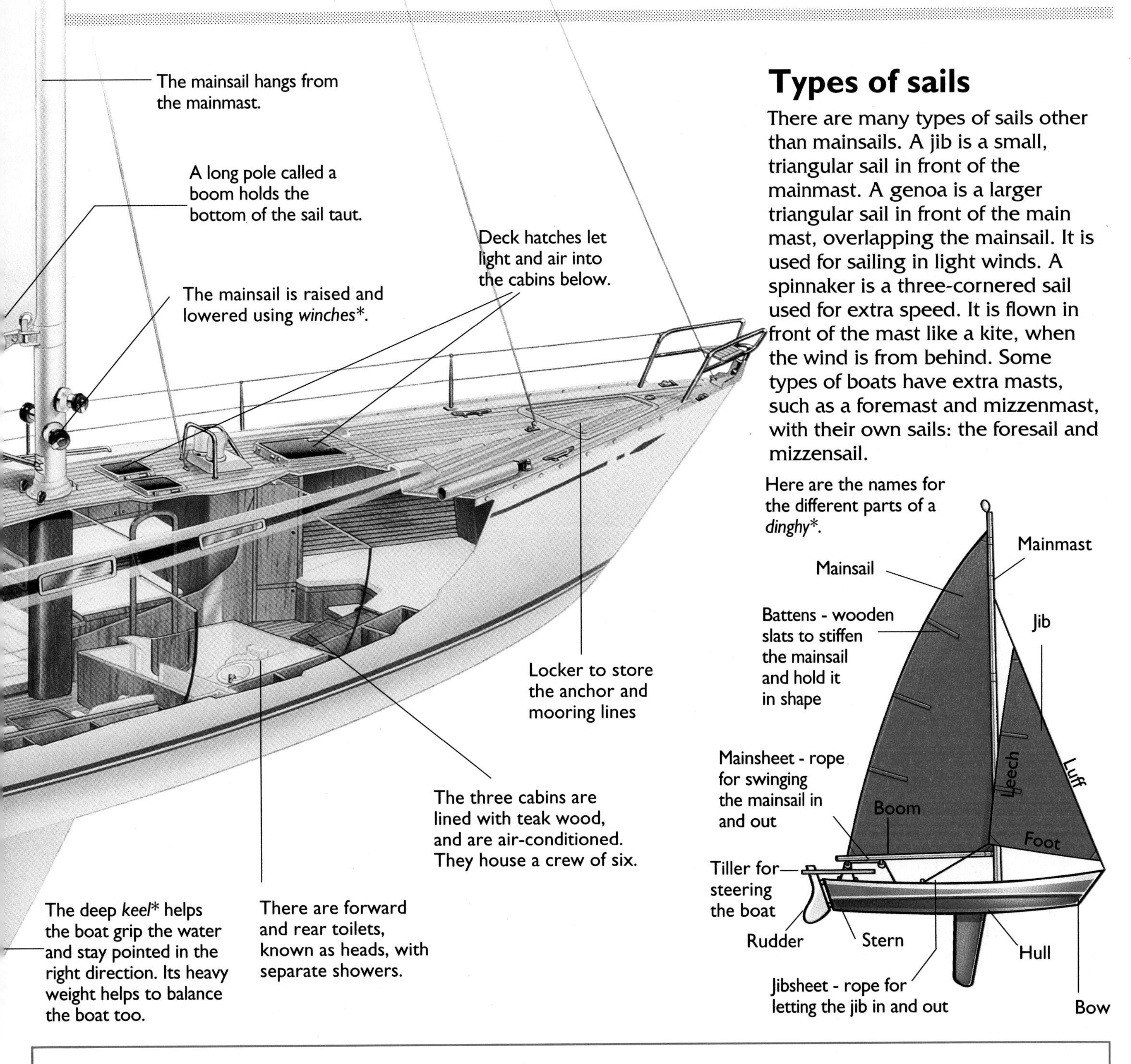

Types of sails

There are many types of sails other than mainsails. A jib is a small, triangular sail in front of the mainmast. A genoa is a larger triangular sail in front of the main mast, overlapping the mainsail. It is used for sailing in light winds. A spinnaker is a three-cornered sail used for extra speed. It is flown in front of the mast like a kite, when the wind is from behind. Some types of boats have extra masts, such as a foremast and mizzenmast, with their own sails: the foresail and mizzensail.

Sailing and wind direction

Boats can sail in any direction, except straight into the wind, or up to 45° either side of it. Within this area (called the "No Go Zone"), sails flap and lose the power to drive a boat forward. So, to sail into the wind, a boa has to zigzag its way forward. This is known as tacking. Here are three ways of using the wind to sail a boat.

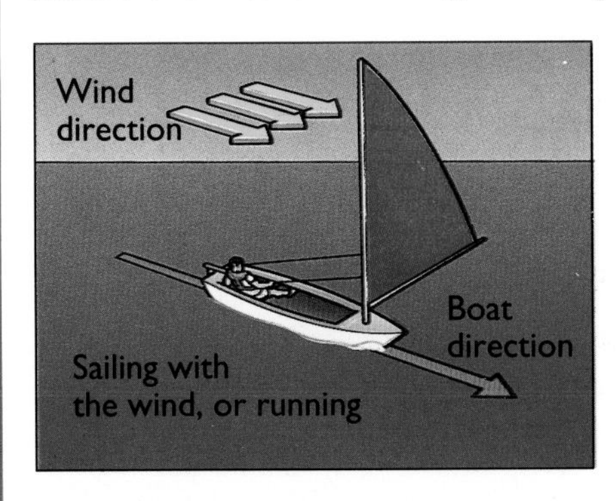

Here, the boat heads in more or less the same direction as the wind, with the sail set at right angles to it. This is a slow way to sail.

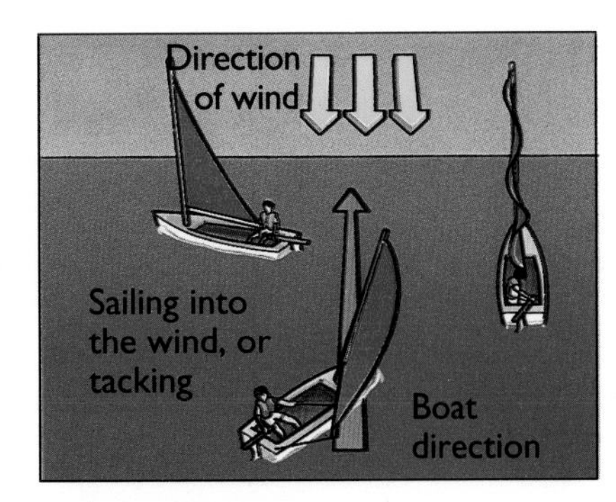

The boat zigzags its way forward at an angle to the wind. It keeps switching the side of the sail that faces the wind to stay on course.

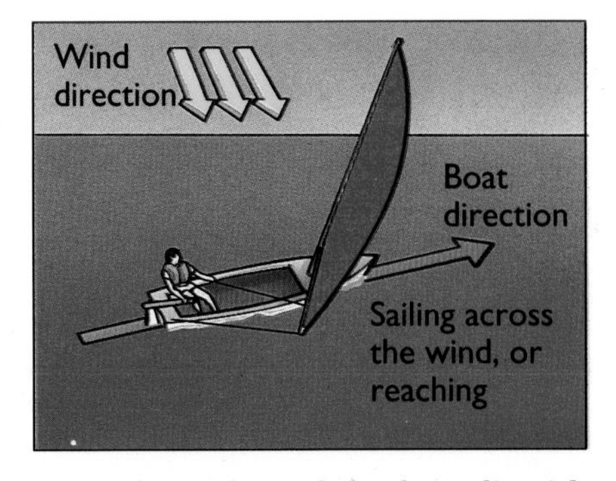

Both the sails and the boat lie side-ways to the wind. This is a course that traps the wind best and makes for the most speed.

Ferries

Some of the busiest ferry routes in the world cross the English Channel. At the height of summer, over 130 trips a day are made between Calais in France and Dover in England, with ships leaving port every 30 minutes.

From inside, the ferries on this short sea journey look like enormous car parks. Beneath their comfortable passenger areas, they stow hundreds of cars and trucks.

Pride of Calais	
Weight:	26,500 tonnes (25,970 tons)
Length:	170m (558ft) (as long as 1 1/2 soccer fields)
Width:	28m (92ft)
Speed:	22 knots
Crew:	110-120 per shift

Pride of Calais

On a single trip from Dover to Calais, the *Pride of Calais* superferry can carry up to 2,300 passengers and 650 cars or 100 trucks. The ship works day and night, all year long. It makes the 42km (26 mile) crossing in about 75 minutes, and usually stays in port for less than an hour before its next trip.

P&O European Ferries

One of the busiest lines in the English Channel is P&O European Ferries. It runs five ships from Dover to Calais, including the *Pride of Calais*.

The *Pride of Calais* and its sister ship the *Pride of Dover* between them carried 5 million passengers in 1995.

Over two million meals a year are served in four different types of restaurants.

Cars and trucks can drive on at one end, park, and then drive straight off at the far end, without ever having to turn or back up.

People in the Club Class lounge have access to phones, faxes, writing desks and photocopiers, so they can work as they travel.

The main diesel engine sits below the car deck.

Electronic eyes

In crowded waters, fishing boats and yachts sail by every day. The heavy traffic keeps a captain alert even in fine weather. But at night, or in fog or storms, the only way to see what's out there is by radar. The long whirling bars at the top of ferry masts are radar antennae. They can see ships, islands, marker buoys and even landmarks on the coast.

1. Radar signals are broadcast from the ferry some 500 times a second. They travel at the speed of light.

2. If they hit a ship 3 km (18.6 miles) away, a faint echo bounces back.

3. The signals are reflected back 1/500th second later.

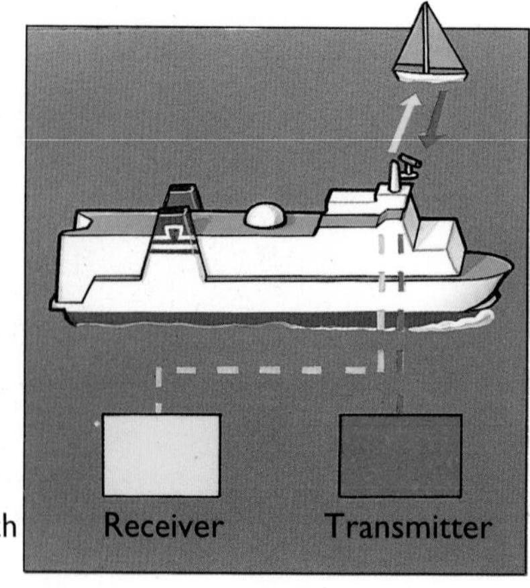

Ship on screen

The receiver turns the echo into a bright light on the radar screen. The navigator uses this to track the direction, speed and distance of the ship and steers a course to avoid it.

Roll-on, roll-off

The vehicle decks have wide bow and stern doors, and huge open parking spaces. This means that hundreds of vehicles can drive in and out swiftly with ease, so loading never takes long. This arrangement is known as roll-on, roll-off, or ro-ro.

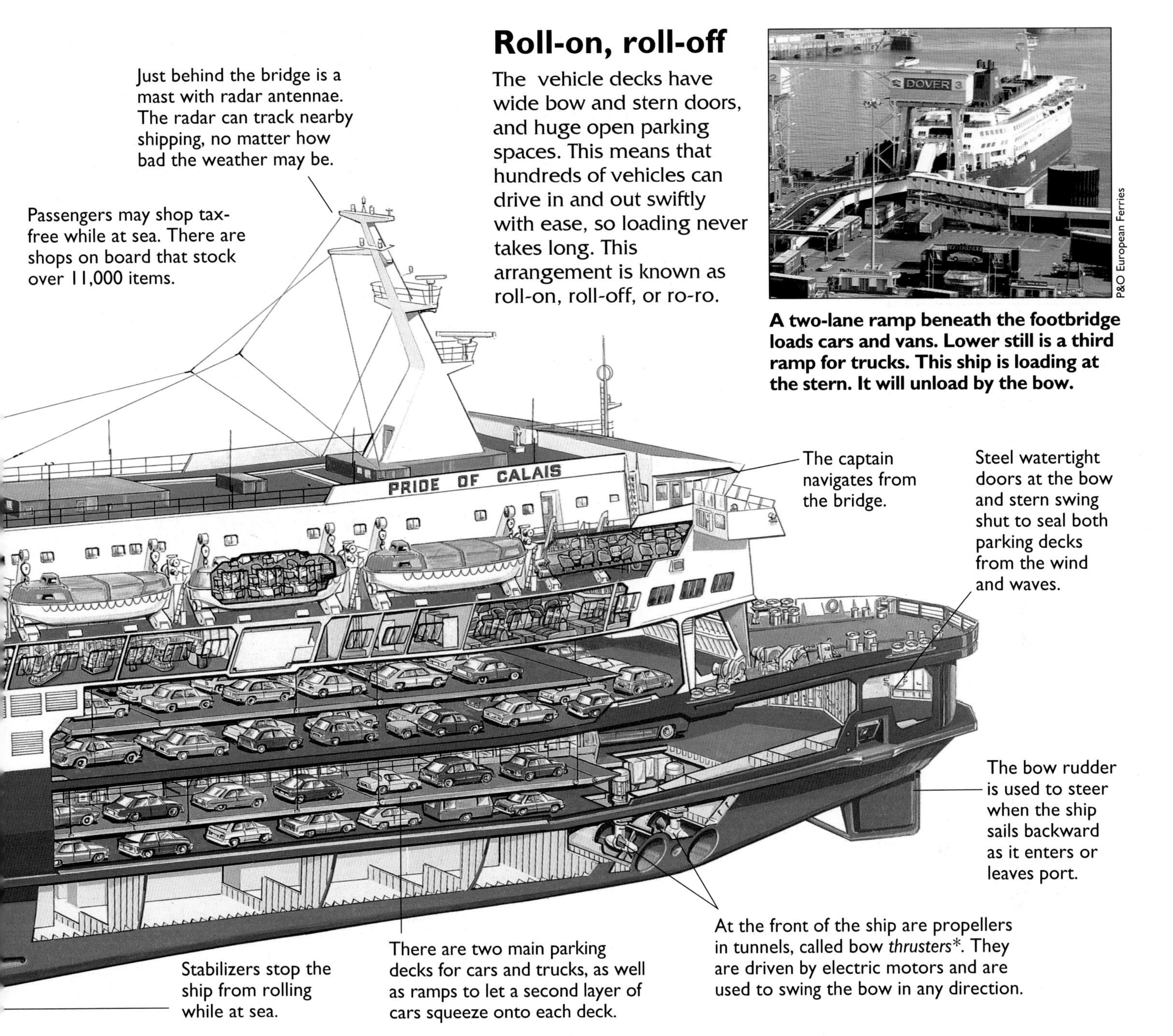

A two-lane ramp beneath the footbridge loads cars and vans. Lower still is a third ramp for trucks. This ship is loading at the stern. It will unload by the bow.

Air-cushioned vehicles

Ferries that use a powerful cushion of air to lift themselves off the ground are called air-cushioned vehicles, or ACVs. ACVs can hover in one place, or move forward, backward and sideways. They can cross water, mud, sand and level ground, which means that they are able to fly from shore to shore without having to use special ports. On a single trip, a big air-cushioned vehicle can take up to 400 passengers and 60 cars.

This ACV is a BHC AP. 1-88. It can carry 101 passengers with a top speed of 92 km/h (56mph).

This thruster blasts a jet of air out. It can turn left and right and helps steer the craft.

The captain, navigator and flight engineer control the craft from the flight deck.

Four propellers push the craft along, and swivel around to help it turn sideways.

The anti-bounce web helps support the skirt. Holes allow air in, but not out of, the outer chamber.

The outer chamber is kept full of air. This keeps the craft stable in rough weather.

Large fans suck in air to fill the skirt.

Air is blown down through a flexible rubber skirt to form a cushion that lifts the vehicle gently off the ground.

Flexible flaps at the bottom of the skirt help the craft travel over rough surfaces, while trapping the air beneath it.

Engines

The engines of modern vessels range in size, from tiny outboards a child can lift, to diesels the size of a room and gas turbines as powerful as the jets on an airliner.

Some marine engines run on a mixture of petrol and oil, others use diesel fuel. Most are designed to run at a steady speed for long periods of time while the vessel cruises. Stop-start driving (such as a car faces in traffic) is unusual. Engines mostly drive propellers that range from the size of your hand, to about 7m (23ft) across in the case of supertankers. On some fast ships, engines drive water jets instead, because they reach much higher speeds with less wear and tear.

Electric power

This Yamaha electric drive outboard engine can propel a small boat with hardly any noise. It weighs less than 9 kg (20lbs), runs on a 12-volt car battery and produces 1/3 *horsepower** of thrust. It's perfect for watching wildlife, or finding fish without disturbing them.

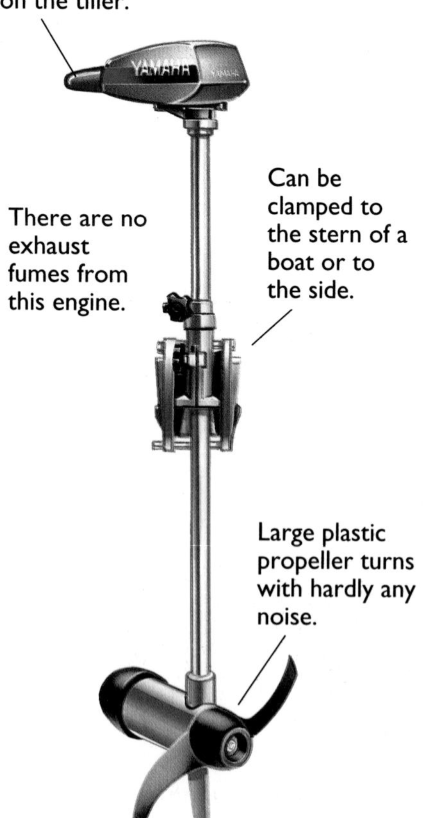

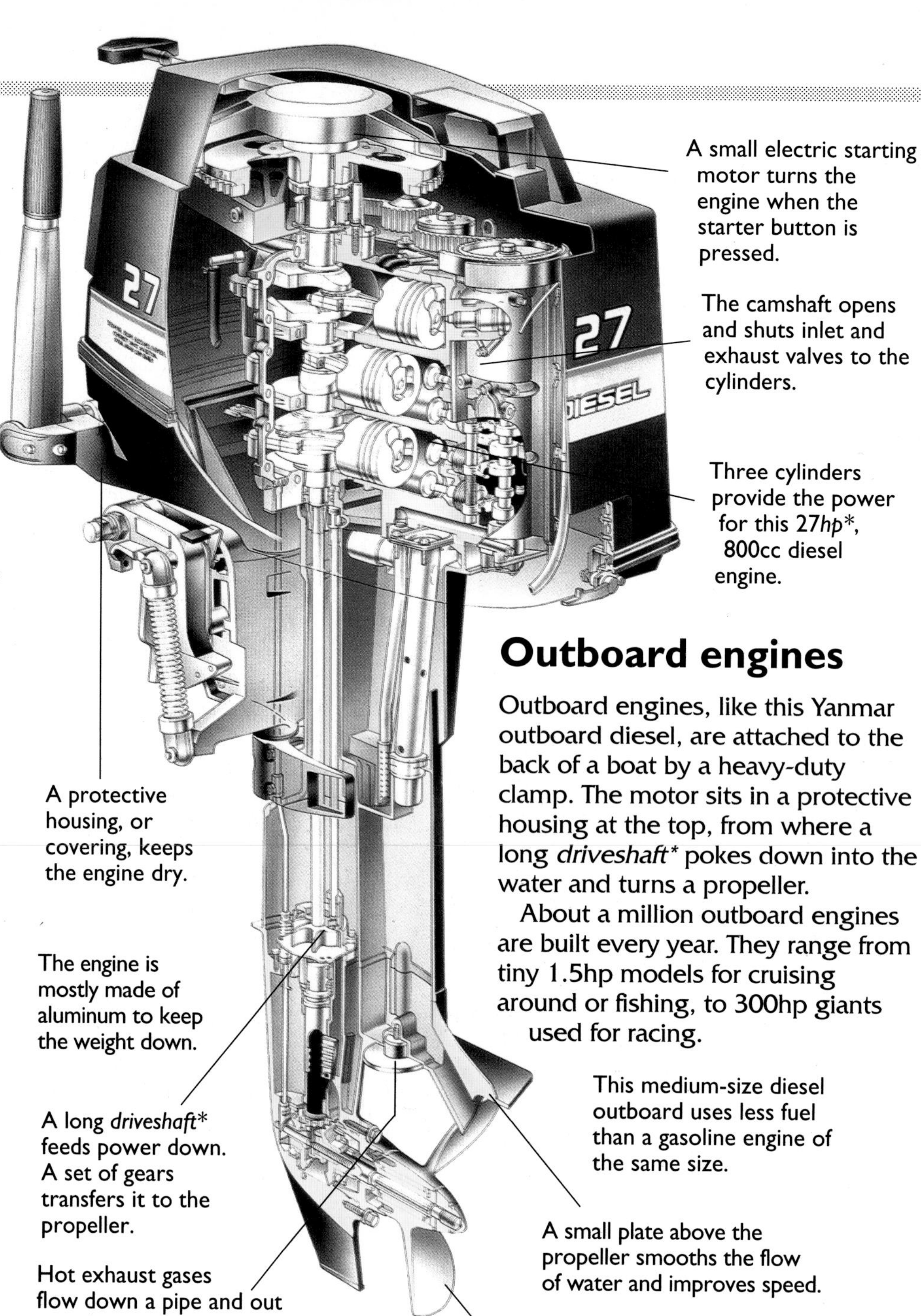

Outboard engines

Outboard engines, like this Yanmar outboard diesel, are attached to the back of a boat by a heavy-duty clamp. The motor sits in a protective housing at the top, from where a long *driveshaft** pokes down into the water and turns a propeller.

About a million outboard engines are built every year. They range from tiny 1.5hp models for cruising around or fishing, to 300hp giants used for racing.

How do propellers push?

As they spin, propeller blades force water to rush backward. The flow creates a strong thrust that shoves a boat forward. Big, slow-turning propellers have the strongest thrust of all.

Because propeller blades are curved, like those of a plane engine, water flows faster over the front of the blade than the back. This creates a second strong force, of *suction**, that also pulls the propeller forward as it turns.

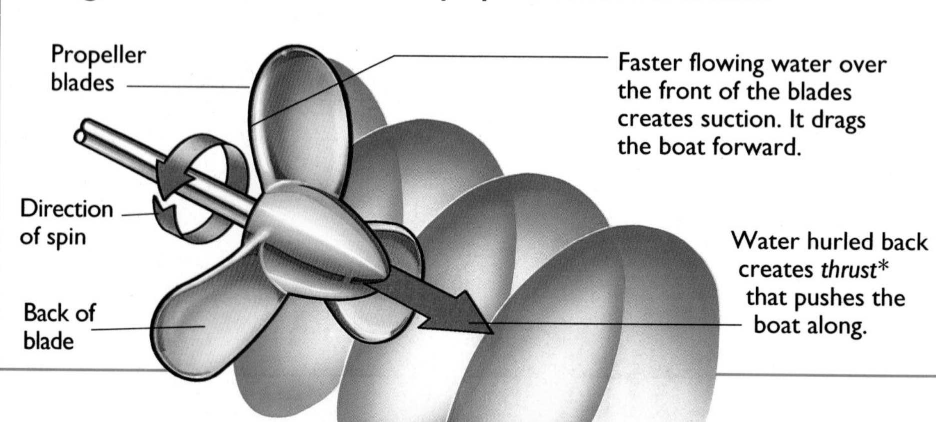

Inboard engines

Inboard diesel engines are the workhorses of the sea. They are used by yachts, fishing boats and all kinds of work boats, from tugs to supertankers. They are tough, strong, thrifty with fuel and can run for hours with next to no servicing.

This small diesel engine is used by sailing yachts to motor in and out of port, or to cruise when the sails are down. It runs quietly and smoothly and is extremely reliable.

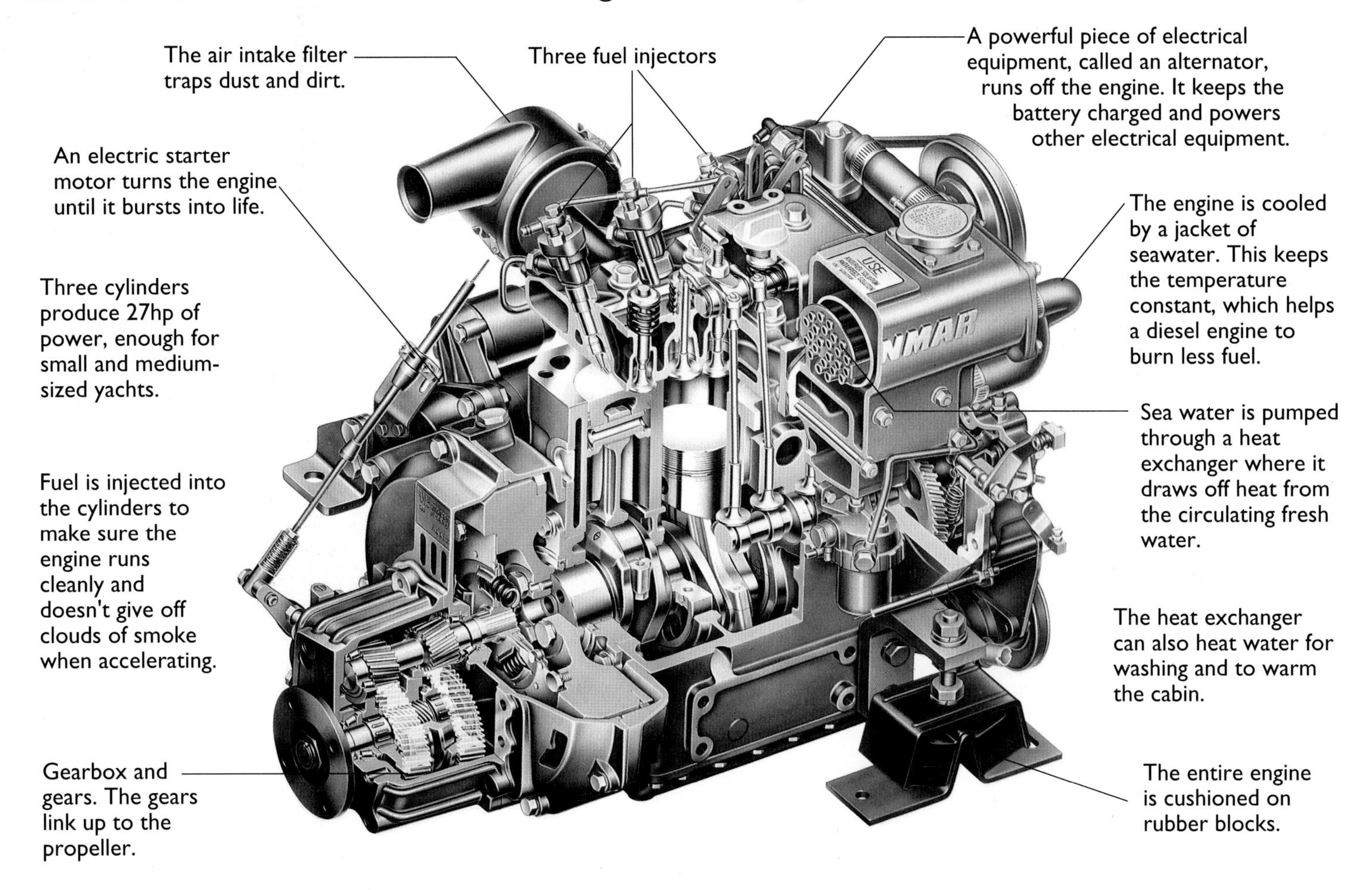

Turbine engines

Ships which need to travel fast (ferries, ACVs and warships) all have gas turbine engines. Turbines allow a boat to go faster because of their small size and light weight. (They can be up to 80% lighter and 60% smaller than diesel engines of the same power.) The gas turbines found in ships are versions of the same engines that power jet planes.

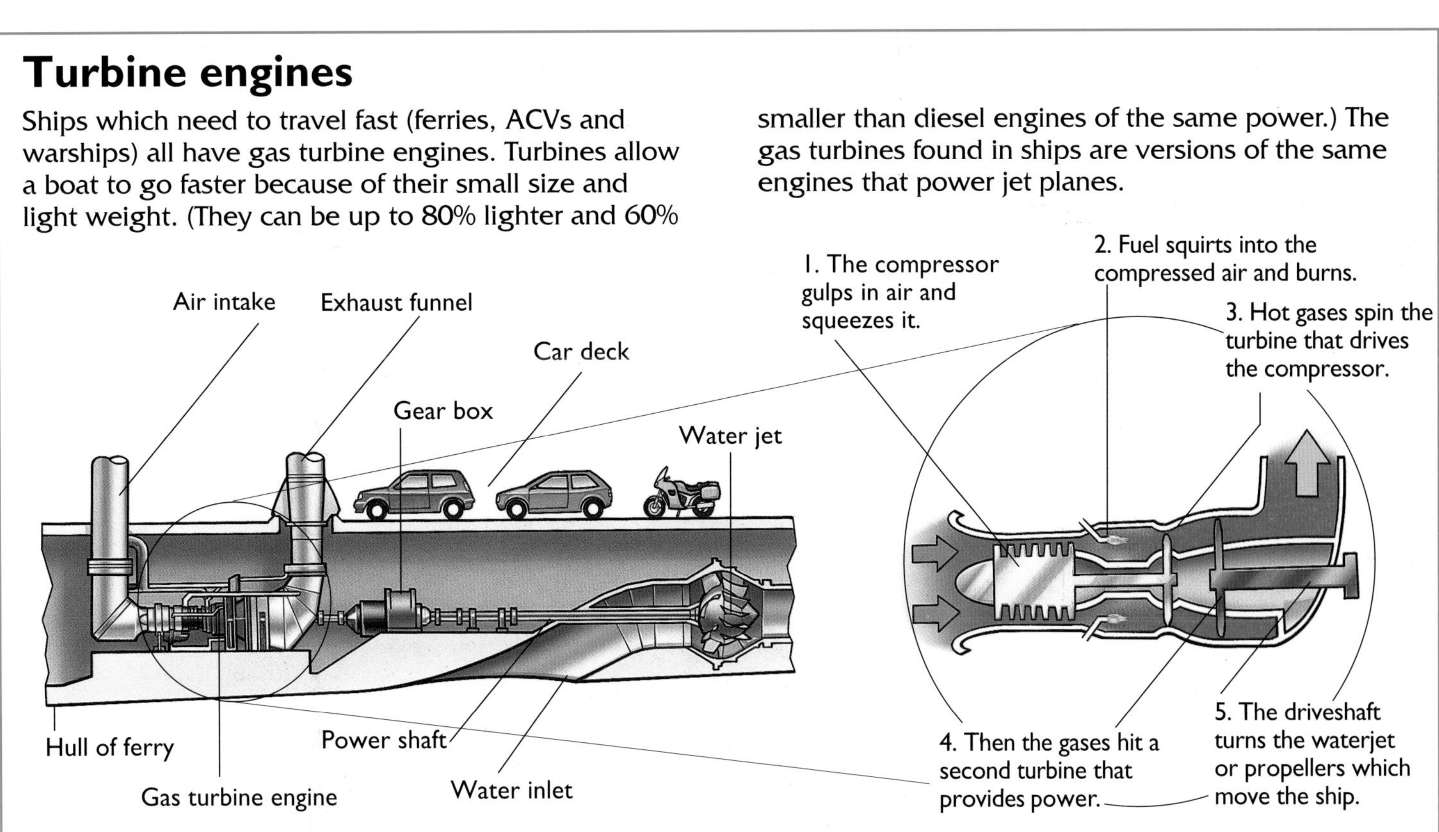

Lifeboats

Lifeboats are some of the toughest working boats in the world. They are built to go to sea in really foul weather, and to work in waters strewn with rocks and sandbanks. Bucking high winds and breaking seas, they steer right alongside stricken ships to pass towlines or lift off crew.

Trent Class lifeboat

Some of the busiest shipping lanes in the world are next to Britain and Ireland. Apart from oil tankers, cargo ships and ferries, thousands of small fishing boats and yachts go to sea every day. Each year, lifeboats are called out over 6000 times (that's some 16 launches a day), saving more than 1,600 lives. The boats, like the Trent class lifeboat shown here, are all run by the RNLI (the Royal National Lifeboat Institution).

The Trent Lifeboat
Length: 14.26m (46ft 9in)
Weight: 26.5 tonnes (26 tons)
Speed: 25 knots
Range: 400km (250 miles)
Crew: 6
Engines: Two 800hp diesels

Gilbert Hampton

This RNLI Trent class lifeboat covers one stretch of coast and up to 80 km (50 miles) out to sea.

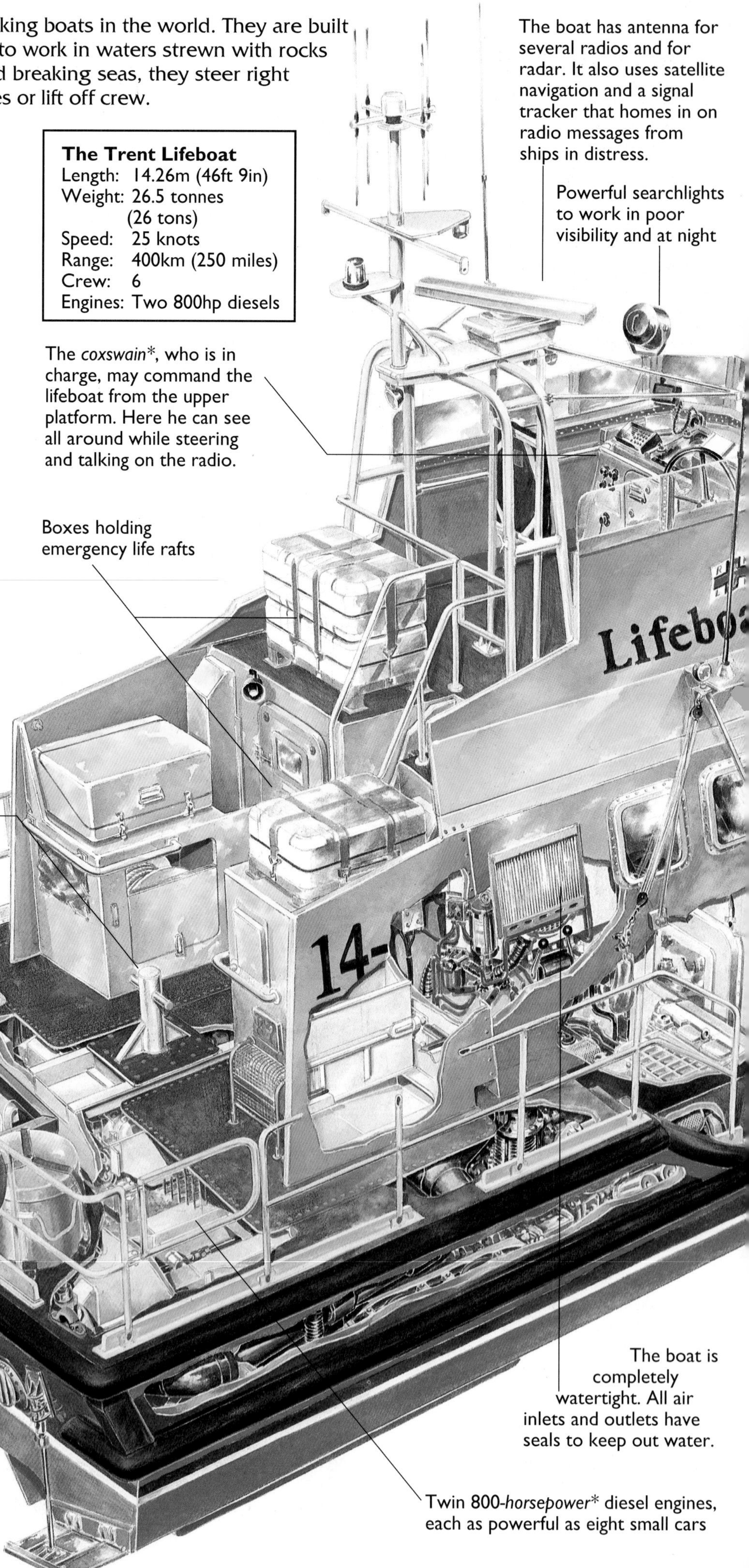

The boat has antenna for several radios and for radar. It also uses satellite navigation and a signal tracker that homes in on radio messages from ships in distress.

Powerful searchlights to work in poor visibility and at night

The *coxswain**, who is in charge, may command the lifeboat from the upper platform. Here he can see all around while steering and talking on the radio.

Boxes holding emergency life rafts

Bollard to fasten rope when towing small boats to safety

Life rings

Rear flaps, called trim tabs, change the angle of the bow to suit sea conditions.

The boat is completely watertight. All air inlets and outlets have seals to keep out water.

The hull has three water inlets. Water flows into two of them to cool the big engines. The third feeds a fire pump in the engine room.

Twin 800-*horsepower** diesel engines, each as powerful as eight small cars

The right way up!

Lifeboats are built of tough lightweight materials that are completely watertight. They will bob upright almost at once if a wave ever knocks them flat. As they flip over, their engines automatically slow down. Then, as soon as the boats right themselves, the coxswain simply opens the throttle and continues on his way.

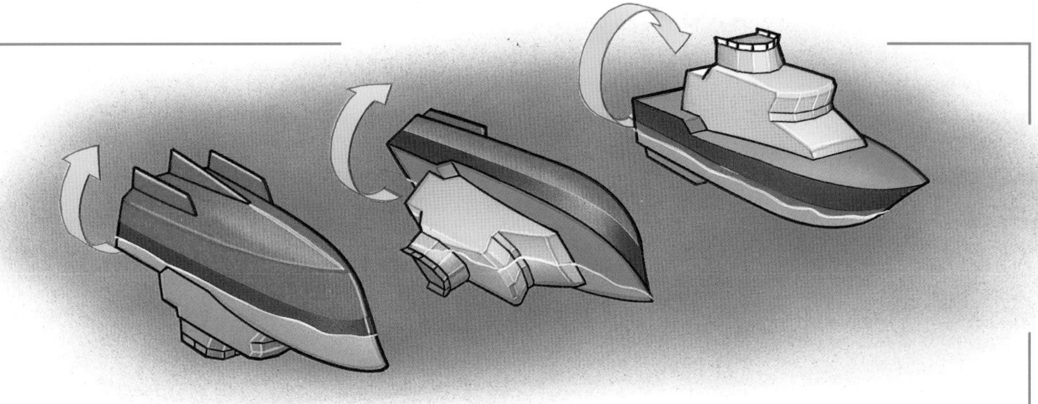

1. All new lifeboats are capsize-tested for safety. A crane tilts the boat into the water until it is lying completely upside down.

2. As the crane lines are dropped, the boat quickly turns itself the right way up. Water pours from the upper decks as it rights itself.

3. The heavy engines are so low down, and there is so much air in the cabin and hull, that the lifeboat flips upright without needing help.

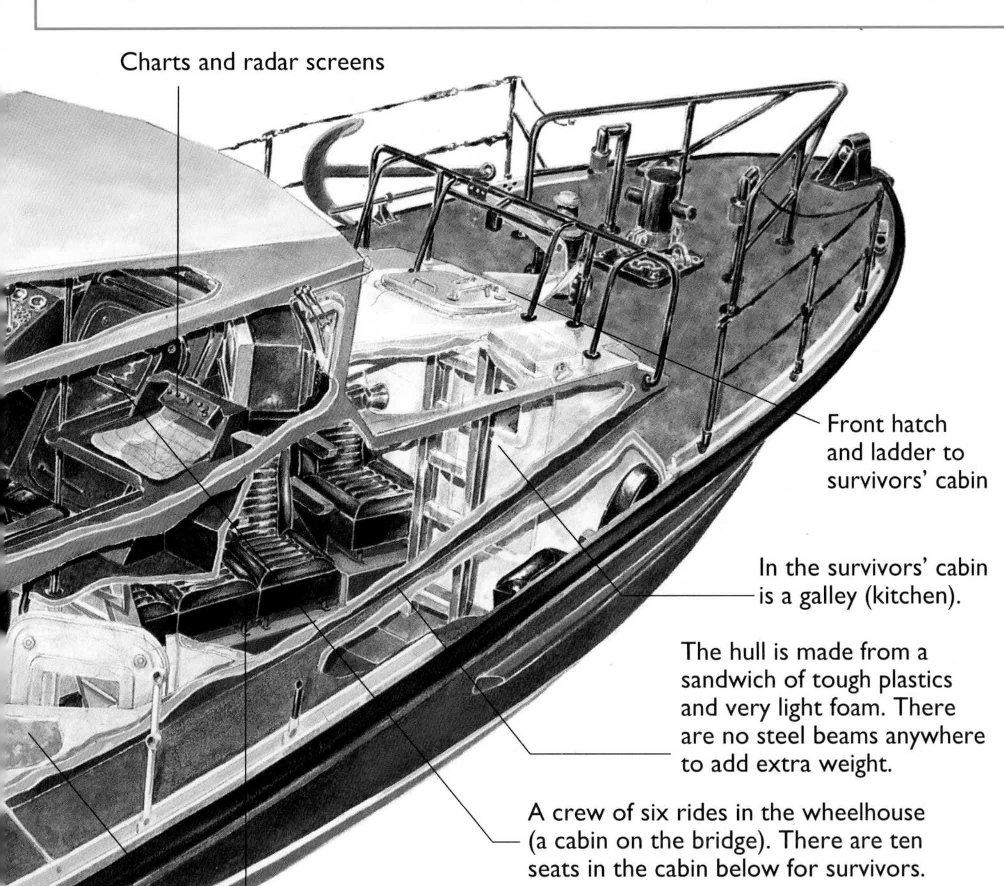

Side keels

A lifeboat may work so close to shore that a really big wave can make it touch bottom. To protect the propellers, it has a pair of very deep keels on either side of the main keel. These reach further down than the propeller blades and so will touch bottom first. They also keep the boat upright at low tide if it gets stranded away from base.

Propellers tucked close to the hull, protected by the keels.

Side keel

Main keel

Side keel

A quick launch

Some lifeboats are moored afloat, but others are stationed in boathouses. In order to put to sea, they use a greased slope called a slipway. First their engines are started. Then, once the single holding wire is released, the lifeboat slides down the slipway and gathers speed. It hits the water at almost nine *knots**.

A groove in the slipway guides the keel.

The side keels keep the lifeboat upright.

Racing boats

Racing powerboats are designed to rise out of the water and skim the surface at high speed. There are three basic types: monohulls, catamarans and hydroplanes.

A monohull is another name for a single-hulled boat. (Most non-racing boats belong to this category.) A catamaran has two narrow hulls, one on each side of the driver. The hulls are set wide apart to make the boat stable. A hydroplane is a half-breed. It has two hulls in front, while the back half narrows into a single hull.

Hull shapes

Monohulls have a flaring V-shape that helps the front section of the hull to rise out of the water at high speed.

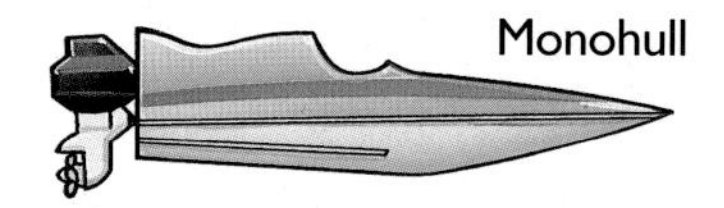

Only the rear hulls of catamarans (and their propeller and rudder) stay wet at race speeds, making them the fastest class of racer.

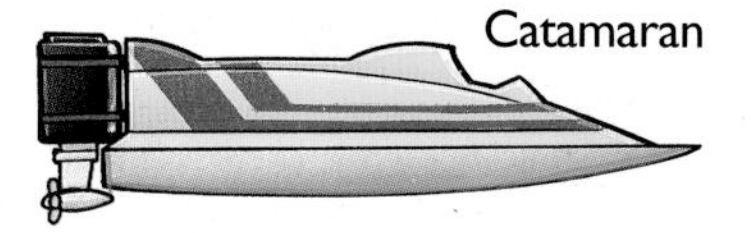

The twin front hulls of hydroplanes create *lift**. At full speed they become airborne. Only the back hull stays in the water.

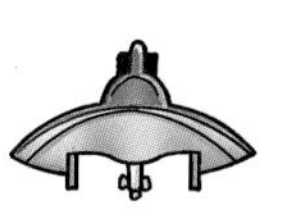

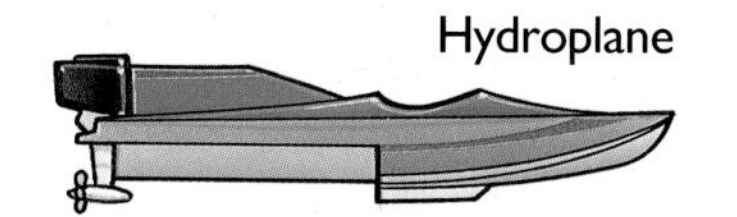

Ocean racer

Surfury was a monohull cruiser designed for offshore races in heavy seas and winds. It was built in 1965 and, over the next five years, carved out a reputation as one of the world's best racers in long distance events.

Two drivers rode half-standing, supported by reclining seats that cushioned them from the battering of high-speed travel over waves.

Part of the cabin roof was replaced with a tarpaulin to save weight.

A third crew member tended the engines. He stood behind the drivers.

Surfury won the British Cowes-Torquay race in 1967 with an average speed of 85km/h (53 mph).

Two big Daytona engines, one behind the other, provided 1050 *horsepower**.

A tiny galley (kitchen) enabled the crew to prepare meals.

Surfury was 11m (36ft) long. It was built from sheets of laminated cedar wood, pressed into shape.

One shaft and propeller, instead of two, cut down *drag** and made the boat much faster.

The front engine's hot exhaust was piped over the side. The rear engine's exhaust was vented through the stern.

Formula 1 racing

Formula 1 boats are small, streamlined catamarans with a huge outboard engine. Their hulls are built from synthetic materials that are light but immensely strong, to withstand pounding at top speeds. Like Formula 1 cars, these boats compete all over the world. There are usually about 12 events a year, held in sheltered waters where boats can reach top speeds of 260 km/h (165 mph).

Chris Davies / Formula Photo

A Victory boat is a type of big catamaran that has won many offshore races in recent years.

Plane speed

Racing boats are built with specially shaped bottoms, so their hulls can plane (or skim) across the surface, rather than carve a path through the water. This increases their speed enormously, because the engines avoid wasting power by having to push aside a heavy weight of water.

Chris Davies / Formula Photo

Circuit racing ranges from Formula I boats to little J250 craft, like this, that children of nine and up can race.

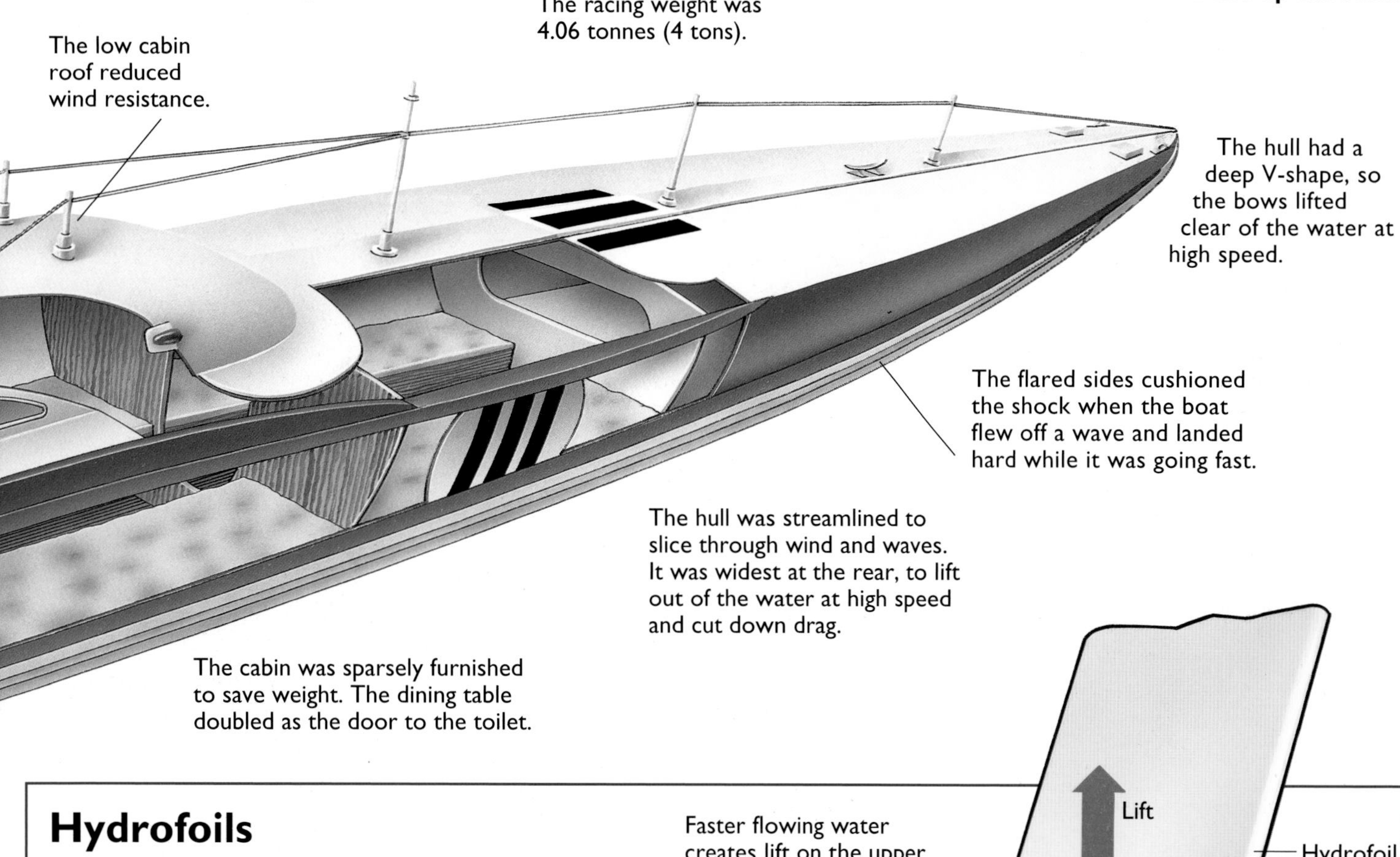

Hydrofoils

The speed of any vessel in water is limited by a force called *drag**, created by the friction between the boat and the water. This means that ordinary boats cannot travel much faster than 35 km/h (20mph). So, with a given size of boat and engine, the easiest way to boost a boat's speed is by lifting the hull out of the water altogether. One of the best ways of doing this is with hydrofoils.

Hydrofoils are flat struts fixed to the hull below water. They are shaped like the wings of a plane. As a boat gathers speed, water flows faster over the curved upper side of a hydrofoil than the flat surface beneath it. Low pressure forms above the foil and, as with a plane wing, creates *lift**. The strut rises up. As the hull lifts out of the water, drag decreases. Now, running with the same power, the boat swiftly picks up speed. Big passenger hydrofoils can accelerate up to more than 90km/h (almost 60 mph).

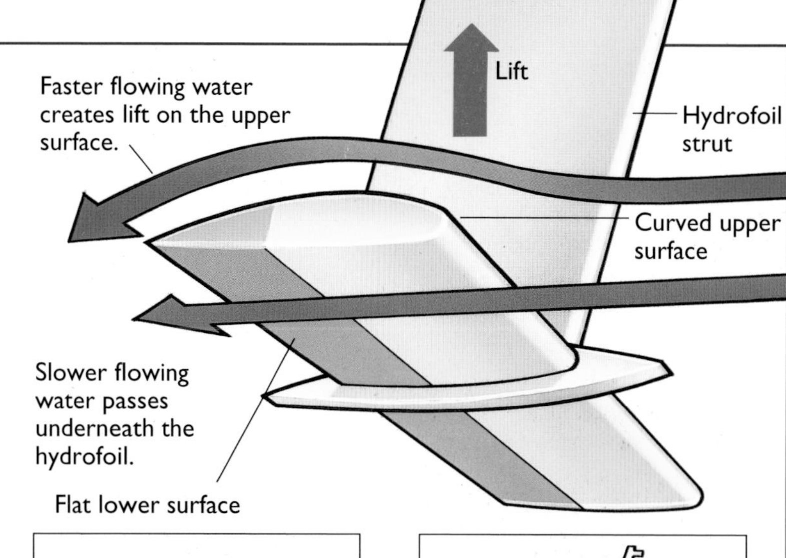

At slow speed, the hull sits in the water like any other boat.

Going fast, the hull rides in the air. Only the foils stay underwater.

Container ships

Modern cargo ships are huge and expensive to build. So they are designed to spend as little time as possible resting in port. To make loading quicker, nearly all freight goes on board in gigantic, prepacked metal boxes, called containers. Other freight is designed to be driven, or towed by trailers, on and off - just like cars on a ferry. This kind of freight is known as roll-on roll-off (or ro-ro). It can include anything from railway carriages to helicopters and earth-moving equipment.

The *Atlantic Companion* (below) is one of five 53,000-tonne (52,000-ton) G3 models owned by the Atlantic Container Line. They are among the largest combination container/ro-ro ships afloat.

The *Atlantic Companion* carries containers and ro-ro cargo from the USA to Europe. Each crossing takes six to eight days.

Atlantic Companion	
Length:	292m (958ft)
Width:	32m (105ft)
Size:	53,000 tonnes (52,000 tons)
Draft:	11m (36ft)
Engine:	27,500 *hp** diesel

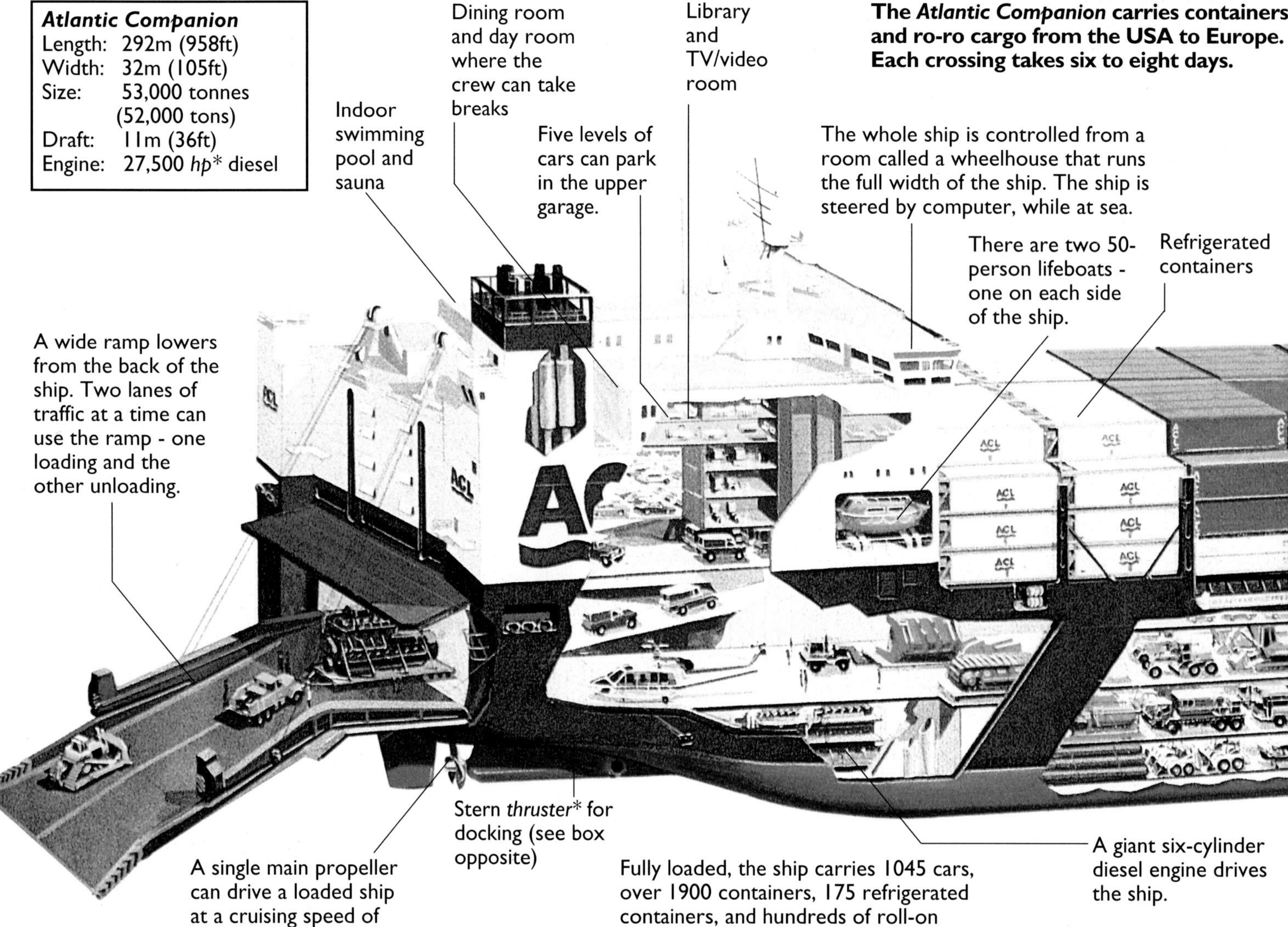

Steering

Almost all ships steer with the help of one or two rudders fixed behind their propellers.

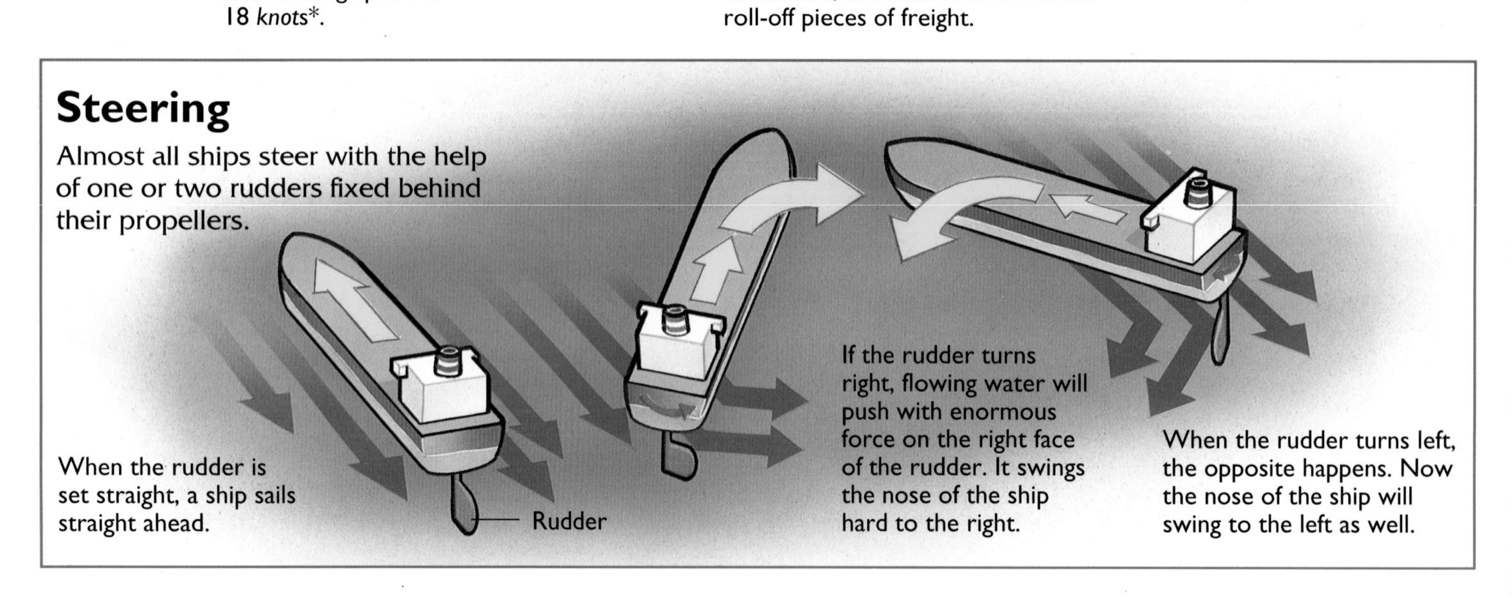

Container ports

Some of the busiest ports in the world, such as Hong Kong and Singapore, each handle over 10 million containers a year.

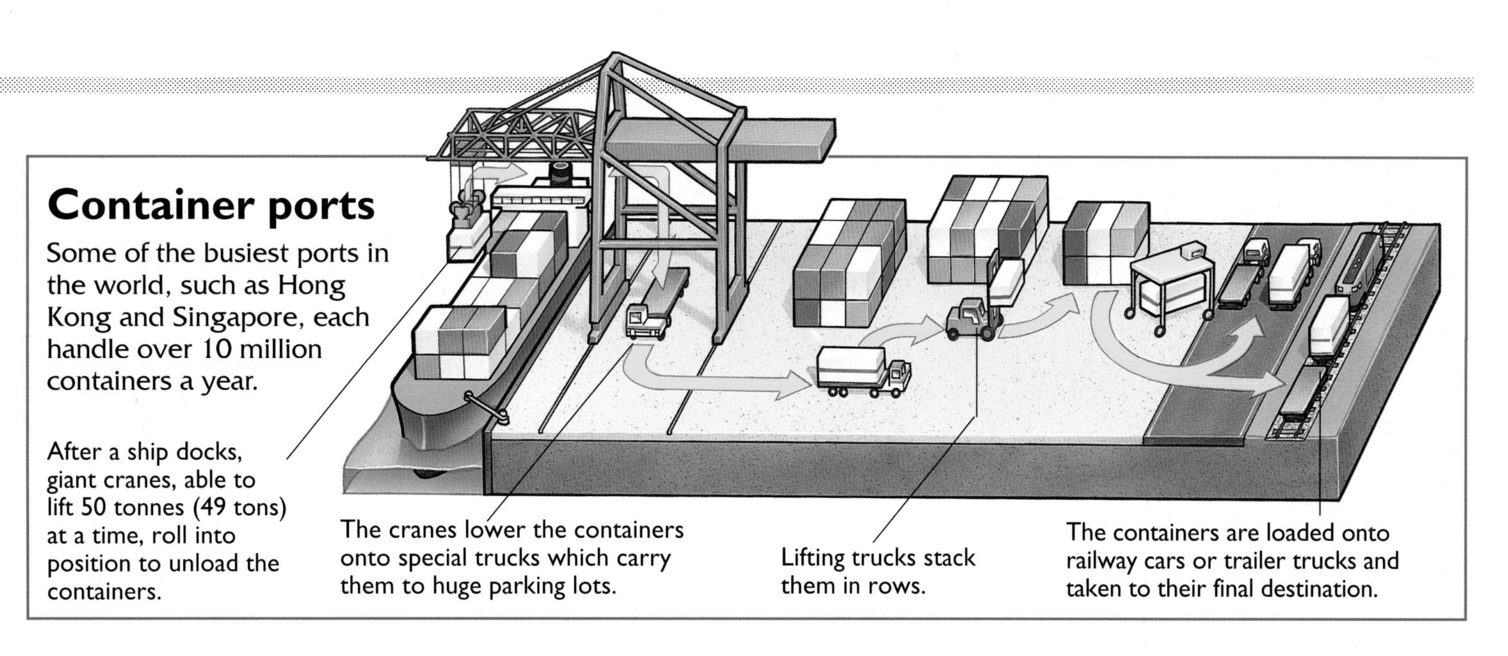

After a ship docks, giant cranes, able to lift 50 tonnes (49 tons) at a time, roll into position to unload the containers.

The cranes lower the containers onto special trucks which carry them to huge parking lots.

Lifting trucks stack them in rows.

The containers are loaded onto railway cars or trailer trucks and taken to their final destination.

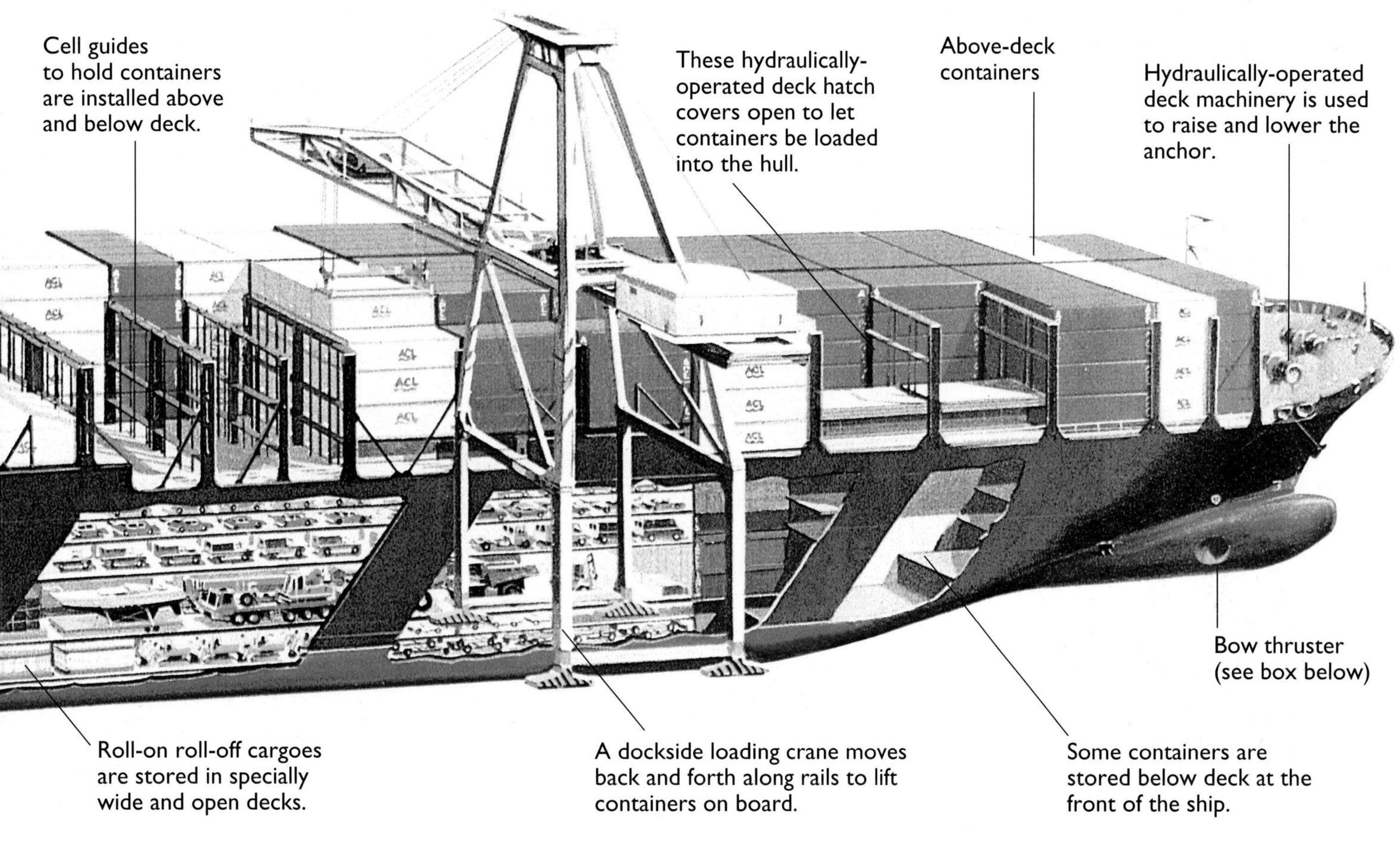

Cell guides to hold containers are installed above and below deck.

These hydraulically-operated deck hatch covers open to let containers be loaded into the hull.

Above-deck containers

Hydraulically-operated deck machinery is used to raise and lower the anchor.

Bow thruster (see box below)

Roll-on roll-off cargoes are stored in specially wide and open decks.

A dockside loading crane moves back and forth along rails to lift containers on board.

Some containers are stored below deck at the front of the ship.

Thrusters

All G3 ships can dock without help from tugboats. They use big propellers, called thrusters, attached to the bow and stern to create a sideways blast of water.

Run together, in the same direction, the thrusters slowly nudge the ship sideways as it docks. Pushing on opposite sides, they turn the ship around within its own length.

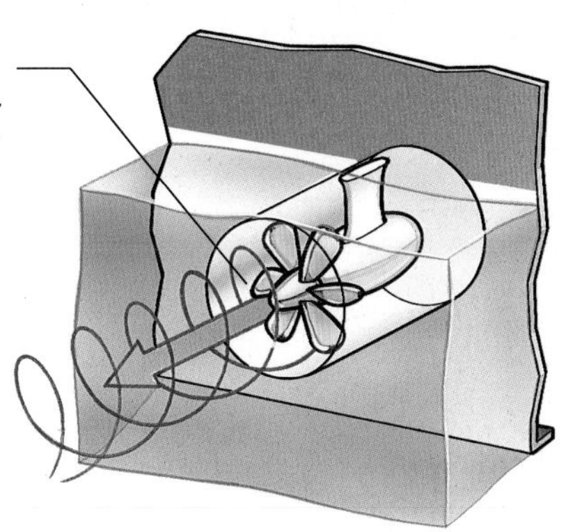

Thrusters work by pushing water from one side of the ship to the other through a large tunnel in the hull.

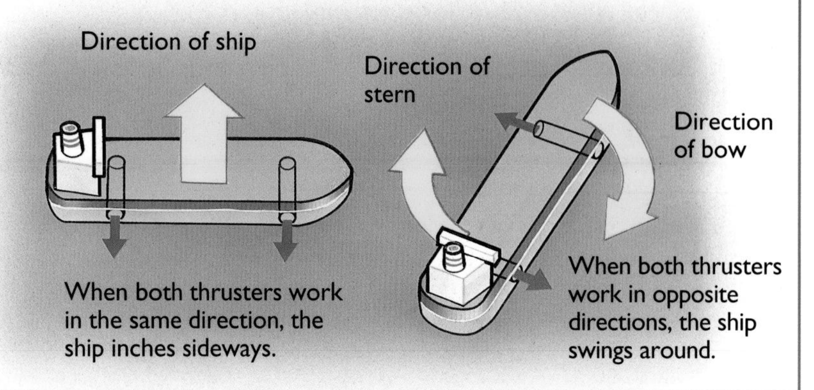

When both thrusters work in the same direction, the ship inches sideways.

When both thrusters work in opposite directions, the ship swings around.

Tugs

Ocean-going ships are so big that they are difficult to steer in enclosed waters. This means they have trouble sailing in and out of port. That's where tugs come in.

Tugs are stubby little boats that stop, start and turn with ease. They handle so well they can work in even the tightest spaces, alongside piers, or in closed-off sections of canals or rivers called locks.

Tucked into a tug's hull is an incredibly powerful engine that drives a huge propeller. This provides the power to tow cargo ships and oil tankers well over a hundred times as heavy as the tug.

A 20 year-old tug

Length:	32m (105ft)
Draught:	4.7m (15ft)
Engines:	Twin diesels
Top speed:	About 12 knots
Crew:	Up to 12
Pulling power:	Around 40 to 50 tonnes (39-49 tons)

All-purpose tugs

A general purpose tug doesn't work only with ships. It may also tow barges and dredgers, fight fires (see right) with its pumps and hoses, or mop up oil spills left by tankers. Tugs are sometimes hired to carry crews and other passengers from ship to shore, or as rescue craft to help ships that get into trouble.

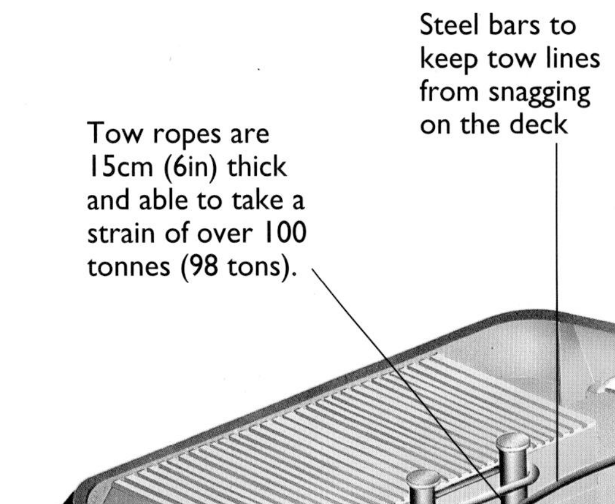

Howard Smith (London) Ltd

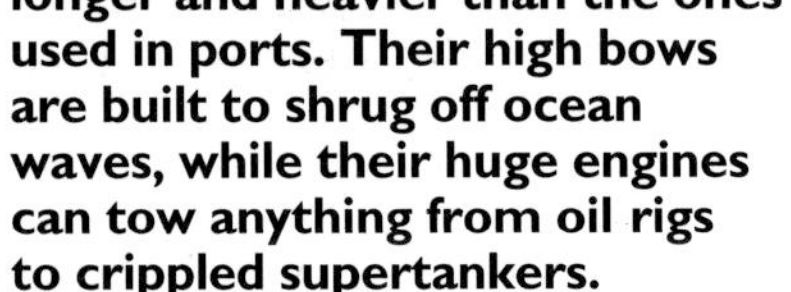
This is a deep-sea tug, which is longer and heavier than the ones used in ports. Their high bows are built to shrug off ocean waves, while their huge engines can tow anything from oil rigs to crippled supertankers.

Propeller power

Many new tugs have two sets of special high-powered propellers called Voith-Schneider propellers. They look a little like egg-beaters, and sit mid-hull instead of at the stern. Unlike ordinary propellers, they can thrust in any direction. This lets tugs tow at full power in whatever direction the captain wants to go.

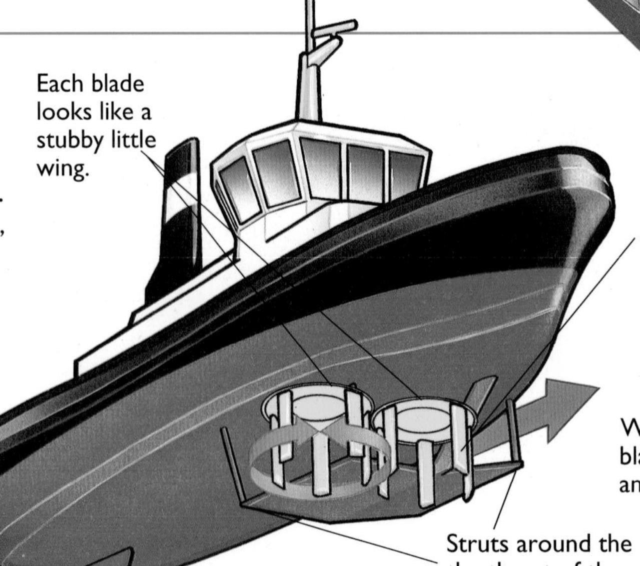

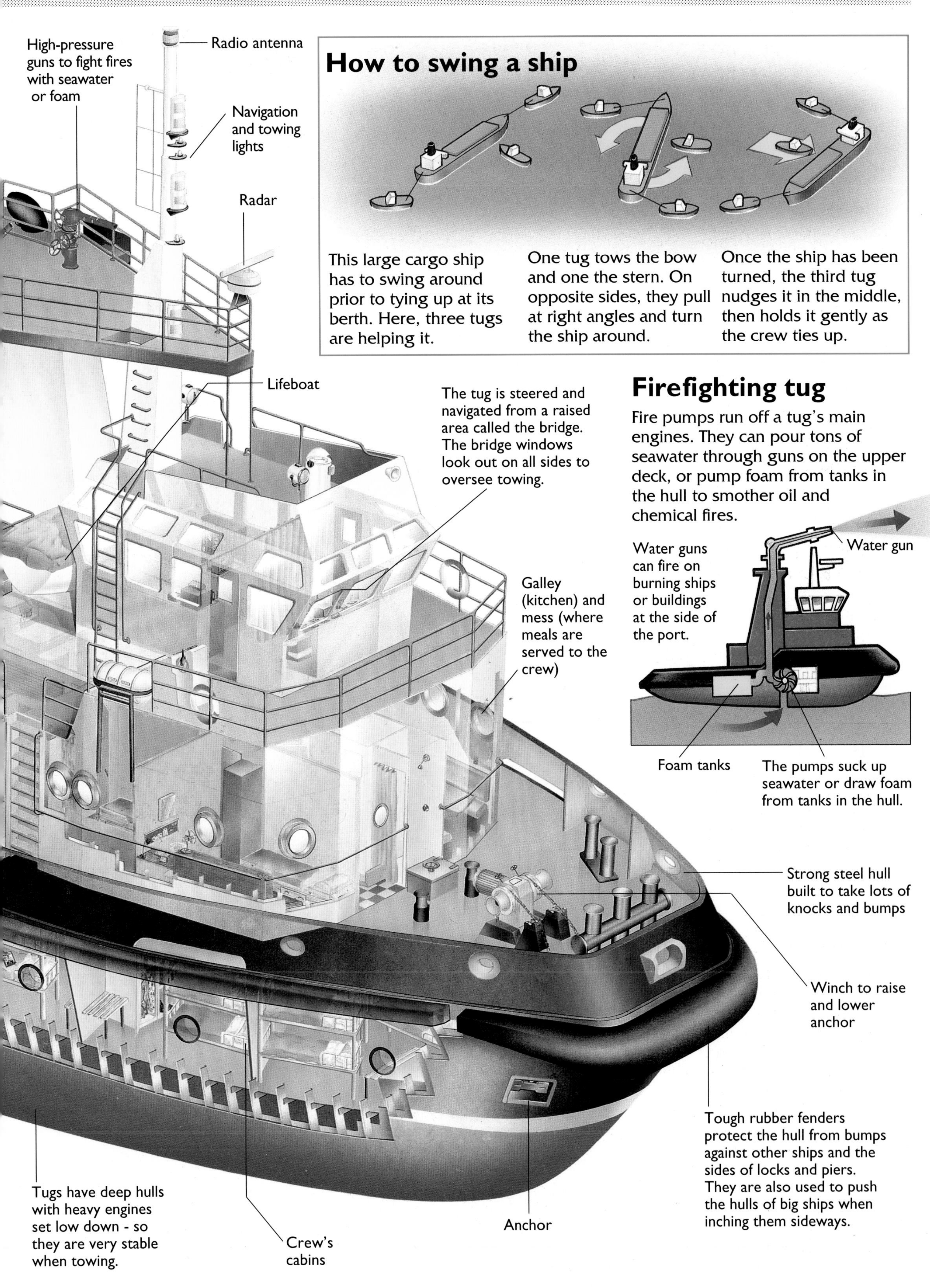

How to swing a ship

This large cargo ship has to swing around prior to tying up at its berth. Here, three tugs are helping it.

One tug tows the bow and one the stern. On opposite sides, they pull at right angles and turn the ship around.

Once the ship has been turned, the third tug nudges it in the middle, then holds it gently as the crew ties up.

Firefighting tug

Fire pumps run off a tug's main engines. They can pour tons of seawater through guns on the upper deck, or pump foam from tanks in the hull to smother oil and chemical fires.

Cruise ships

Few people cross oceans by ship any more. Planes are much faster and more convenient. Although ocean liners have long gone, their place has now been taken by cruise liners. These ships are designed specifically for pleasure trips, usually calling at a number of different ports.

The *Sun Princess*

The *Sun Princess, launched in 1995,* is one of the newest big ships to join the fleet that sails the Caribbean in winter and the Alaska Coast in summer. Cruise ships take over 4.5 million people on trips every year.

At 78,250 tonnes (77,000 tons) and 261m (856ft), the *Sun Princess* is the biggest cruise ship afloat.

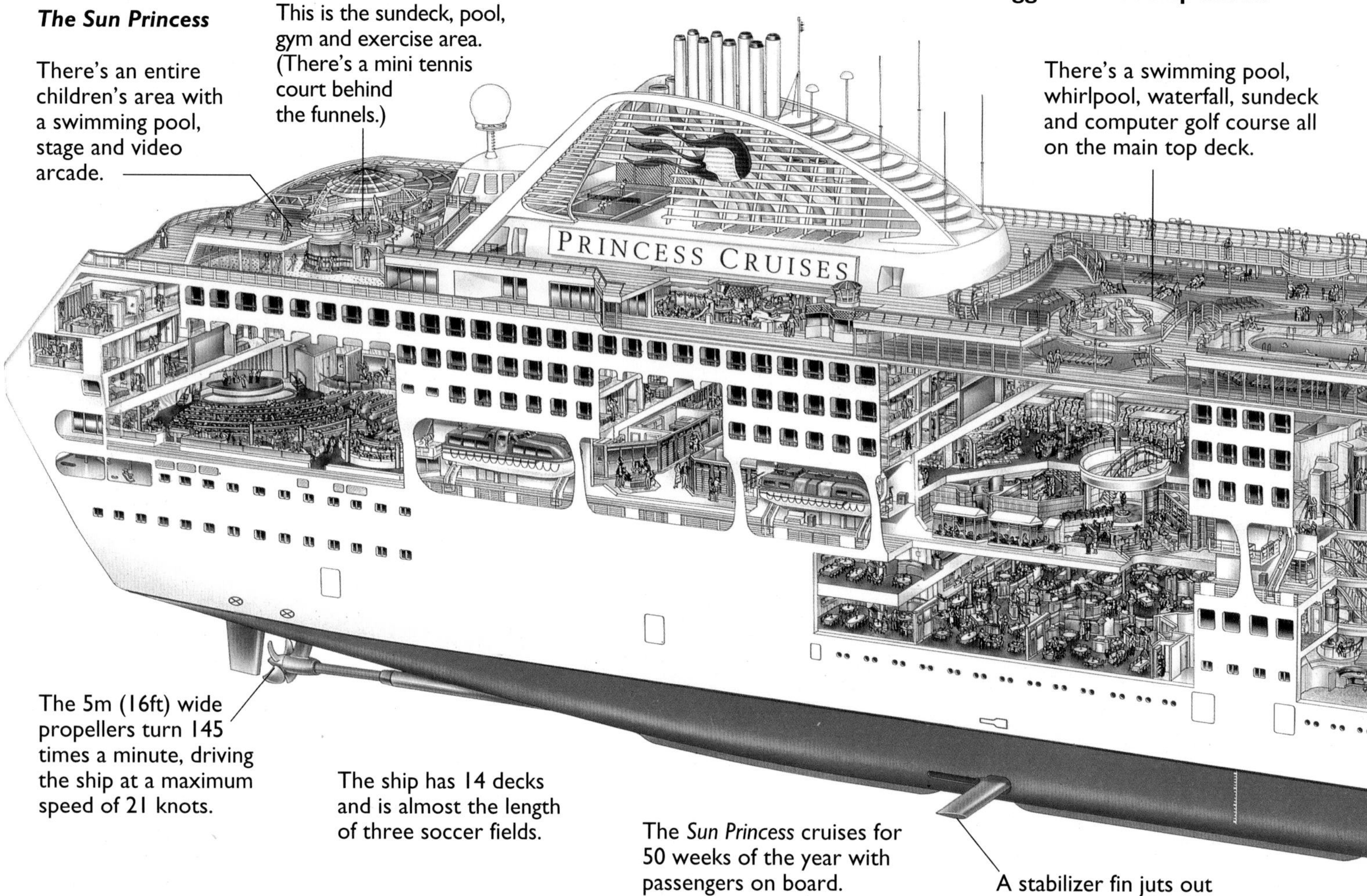

Silent night

The cruising speed of the *Sun Princess* is 21 knots (a good 10 knots slower than older passenger liners like the *QE2*). Its two propellers each have six curved blades, which draw water past the hull with little turbulence. Each propeller is driven by an electric motor, mounted on rubber to cut down noise.

How stabilizers work

Two stubby wings called stabilizers poke from the hull of the ship below the water line. They smooth out the rolling motion of the waves.

These wings waggle back and forth all the time, controlled by computers in the ship that sense exactly what the waves are doing.

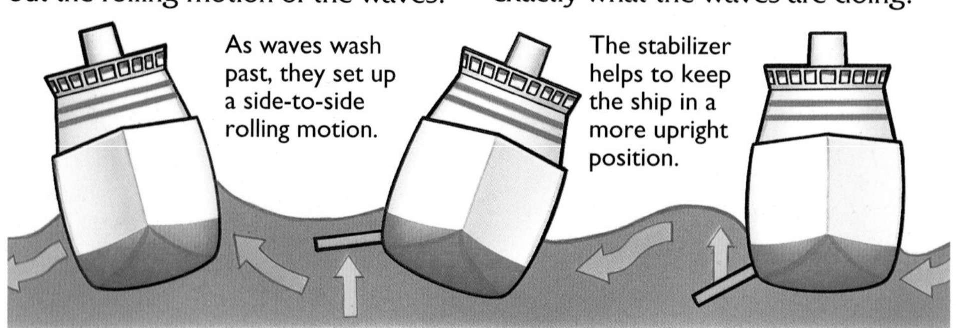

The stabilizers fold into a bay in the sides when the sea is calm. As the sea gets rougher, a single stabilizer is brought into use.

It acts like the wing of a plane, lifting one side of the ship in the opposite direction to the rolling motion of the waves.

The two opposing rolling motions cancel each other out. This means the ship continues in a steadier, more upright manner.

A floating hotel

Part resort, part luxury hotel, cruise ships are amazingly comfortable. In the best suites, passengers can enjoy marble bathrooms, whirlpool tubs, TVs and private bars. Over 400 cabins come with outside balconies overlooking the sea.

P&O

In the heart of the ship is a four-floor high lobby where people can glide up and down in glass elevators.

Sea fare

With four restaurants and cafés, and five bars scattered around the ship, passengers can eat and drink just about any time, day or night.
A typical shopping list for a seven-day cruise might include the following groceries:

10,886 kg (24,000 lbs) of meat
2994 kg (6600 lbs) of fish
726 kg (1600 lbs) of fresh shrimp
4082 kg (9000 lbs) of potatoes
15,876 kg (35,000 lbs) of fruit
Enough coffee to brew 8865 ltrs (1,950 gallons)

Radar antennae, radio equipment and satellite links for phones, faxes, computers and TV.

The ship can take as many as 2,022 passengers at a time, with a crew of 920.

The bridge, the area from which the captain and his officers run the ship

Computers guide and steer the ship. They can stop her outside a port and hold her steady there without ever needing to drop the anchor.

P&O

SUN PRINCESS

The bulb shaped bow parts the waves to enable the ship to slip through the sea with less effort.

The ship has a large auditorium in the front for shows and concerts.

Bulkheads

The hull of a cruise ship, below the water line, is divided into compartments by watertight walls called bulkheads.These are designed so that if water gets into one compartment it doesn't spread through the ship.

Above this lies the watertight bulkhead deck. No water can rise above it, even if the lower hull is entirely flooded. So, even if a ship is sinking, bulkheads stop it from capsizing (rolling over) due to water rushing to one side. This gives people more time to escape.

The compartments below the bulkhead deck hold the engines, air-conditioning, supplies, laundries, and cabins for the crew.

Bulkhead deck

Bulkheads

All watertight bulkhead doors can be shut by remote control from the bridge.

The ship will still stay afloat, even if two compartments are flooded.

Submersibles

Submarines are built for military use. Navies use them to launch missiles or to sink surface ships.

Submersibles are something altogether different. They are small diving craft built for scientific research, archeology, or to work in oil and mineral exploration. Some map the seabed, others repair pipes and cables, and a few are used for rescue work. They can all dive far deeper (about four times as deep) than any military submarine.

Length:	7.6m (25ft)
Width:	2.4m (8ft)
Engines:	6 small electric *thrusters**
Cruising speed:	1 *knot**
Top speed:	1.5 knots
Max depth:	4000m (13,000ft)
Range:	8 kms (5 miles)

Alvin the submersible

One of the best-known submersibles is a little research vessel called *Alvin*. First launched in 1964, it has since made thousands of dives around the world. It was the first vessel to explore the wreck of the *Titanic*, and to discover belching vents of hot water at the bottom of the sea. These occur where cracks in the seabed have caused heat deep inside the Earth to raise the temperature of water seeping in by hundreds of degrees. In these isolated spots, scientists have found colonies of strange tube worms and shrimps not known anywhere else.

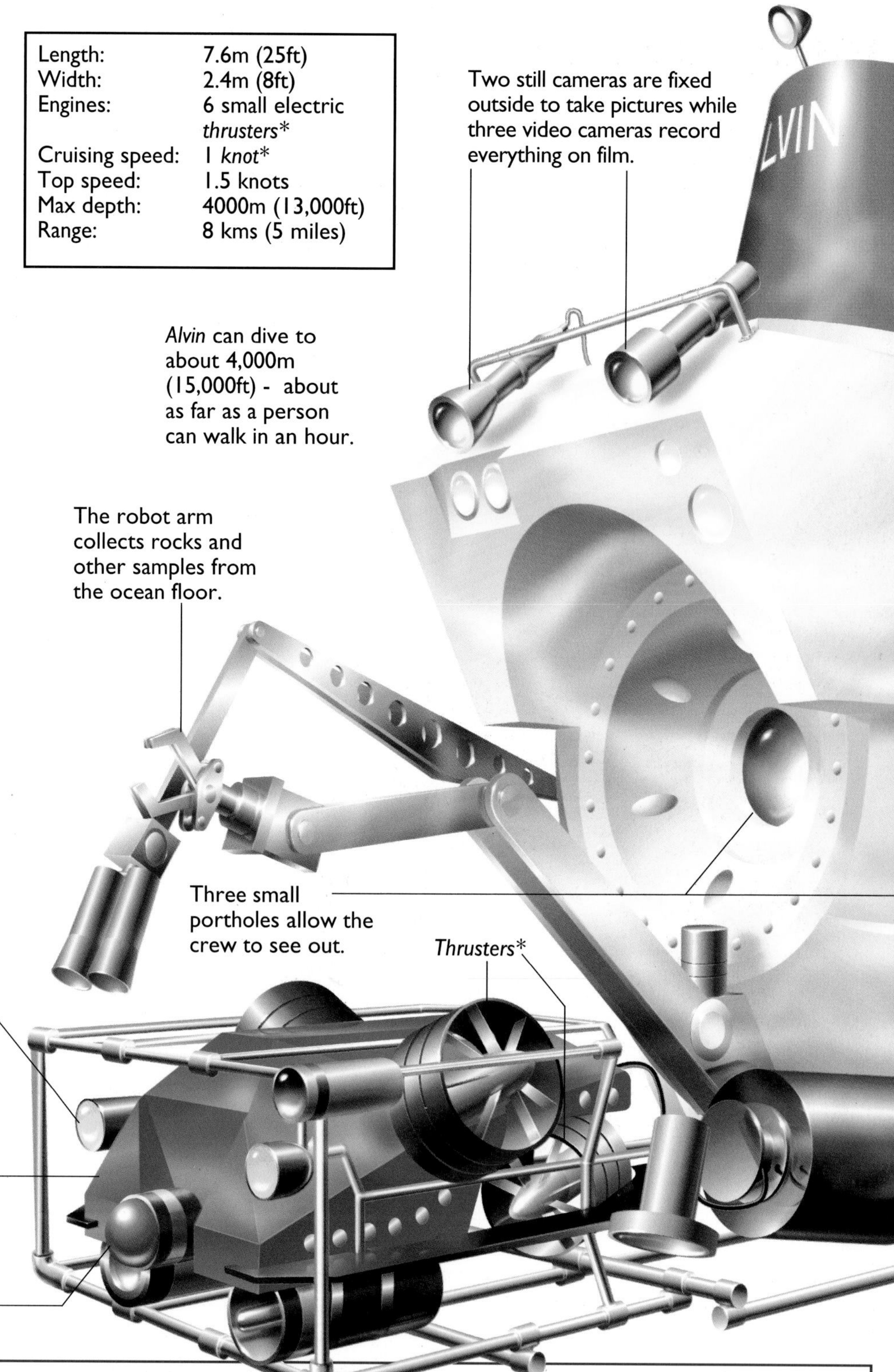

The seafloor where *Alvin* works is pitch black. Its powerful lights can only light up a small patch of seabed.

This is a remote-controlled robot called *Jason Jr*, that was used to explore the wreck of the *Titanic*. It was taken down in a cage, bolted to the front of *Alvin*, and steered by cable into the ship.

Video camera

Using special equipment, divers like this one from *Norbert* can work up to 250m (820ft) deep.

Big squeeze

The amount of air pressure at sea level is called 'one atmosphere'. Underwater, pressure builds up very quickly, as water is far heavier than air. Every 10m (33ft) farther down adds another 'atmosphere' of pressure.

The limit of *Alvin's* range is just under 4,000m (13,120ft). In the deepest parts of the ocean, almost 11,000m (36,000ft) down, pressure may be 1,000 times greater than at the surface. Here a submersible would crumple like an empty can.

Air Pressure and Underwater Pressure

Sea level - 1 atmosphere

10m - 2 atmospheres

4000m - 400 atmospheres (Alvin's limit)

11,000m - 1100 atmospheres

Military submarines

Military submarines are designed to operate in a shallow band of water, no more than about 200-300m (600-900ft) below the surface. They are used to attack surface ships, or hunt enemy submarines and fire missiles. Their hulls are strong, but very few can go deeper than 500m (1640ft).

D. Reynolds / Photo Press

This is a British Trafalgar Class military submarine at anchor. It can reach a top speed of 30 *knots.**

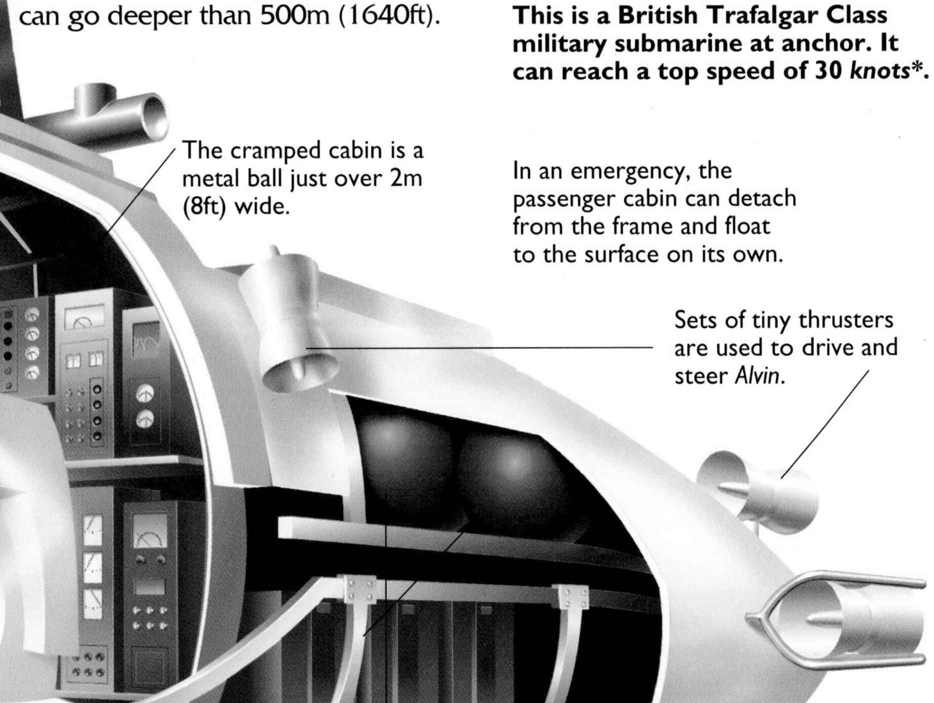

Mini-subs

Mini submersibles are widely used, for example, in the oil business, to move divers, or to work at depths that are too dangerous for free-swimming humans. They are equipped with floodlights, cameras, robot arms, and a highly accurate navigation system so they can find their way about in pitch darkness.

As all these subs run on batteries, they can only stay under for a very short time (usually less than a day) before they surface and recharge.

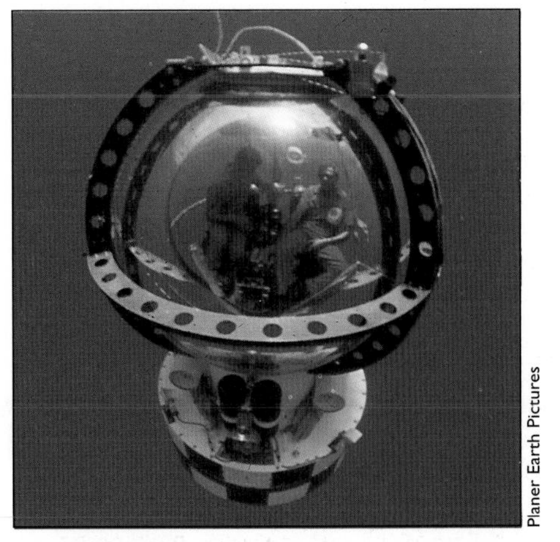

Planer Earth Pictures

***Nemo* (Naval Experimental Manned Observatory) operates at a depth of 183m (600ft), with a crew of two.**

How do subs dive?

Submersibles can only go up and down. They carry heavy lead weights as they dive that are dumped at the bottom when the vessels need to stop going down.

A submarine is different. As well as being able to travel on the surface and dive, it can also hover at whatever depth it wants to. This is possible because it has air tanks, called ballast tanks, all along the outside of its hull. They are open to the sea at the bottom and have vents at the top.

Floating on the surface, the ballast tanks are full of air and their vents are closed.

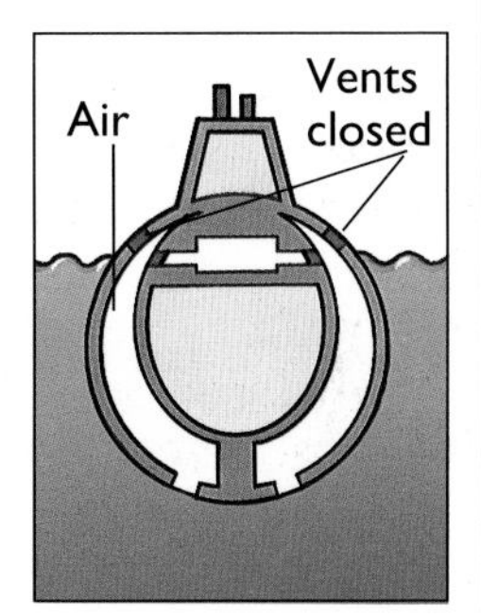

To dive, the vents are opened to let water flood into the tanks. This makes the sub heavier and so it sinks.

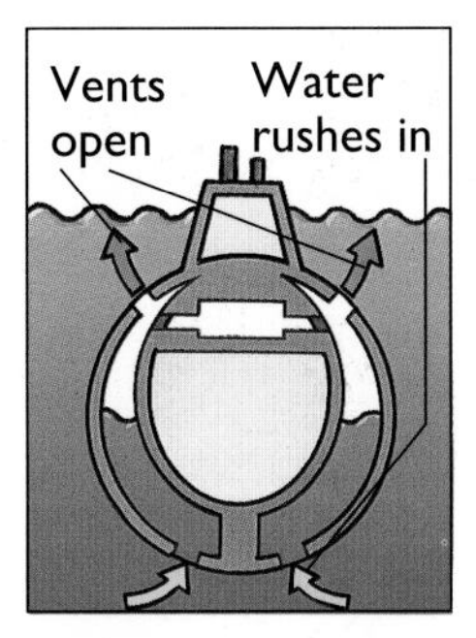

To hover or travel at the desired depth, the vents are closed, so the sub stops sinking. The tanks are full of water.

To go up, high-pressure air is blown into the tanks, forcing out the water. The submarine rises to the surface.

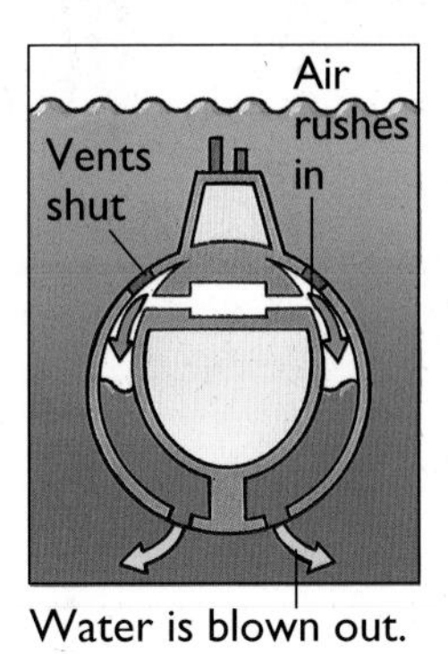

The future

The look of boats has changed out of all recognition in the past 150 years. During this time, they have grown bigger, faster and much more comfortable. If change continues like this, it is likely that boats of the future will look very different from the way they do today. Since the main problem is the way water slows boats down, many of the newest ideas are concentrating on raising them out of the water, to make them go faster.

Air superliner

A group of Japanese companies are testing the idea of fast catamaran freighters, able to carry 1,000 tonnes (984 tons) at over 50 knots, with a range of 800 km (500 miles) or more. One model, the TSL-A, uses a cushion of air to lift much of its body out of the water in order to reach top speed. So far, only half-size models, like the *Hisho* (below), have been tested at sea, but they have been a great success.

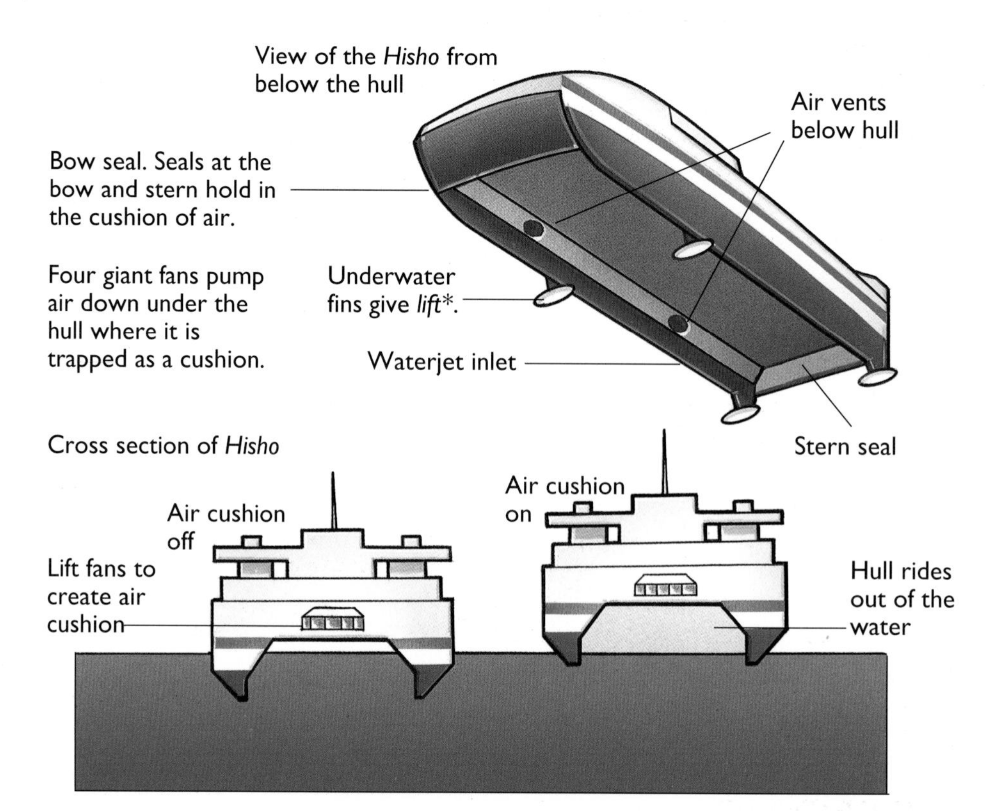

***Hisho* is a 70m (230ft) half-size model of the TSL-A. It is driven by two 16,000hp engines, linked to water jets.**

The boat with no propellers

Japanese engineers have built an experimental boat that runs without propellers or *thrusters**. Instead it is powered by two *superconducting** electromagnetic thrusters. The *Yamato 1* was tested in Kobe, Japan, in 1992, proving that a motor with no moving parts really can work.

The *Yamato 1* has two water tunnels in its hull, wrapped with magnets and electrodes. When these are switched on, they create a force that pushes a jet of seawater through both tunnels and out at the stern with enough power to drive the boat along at eight knots.

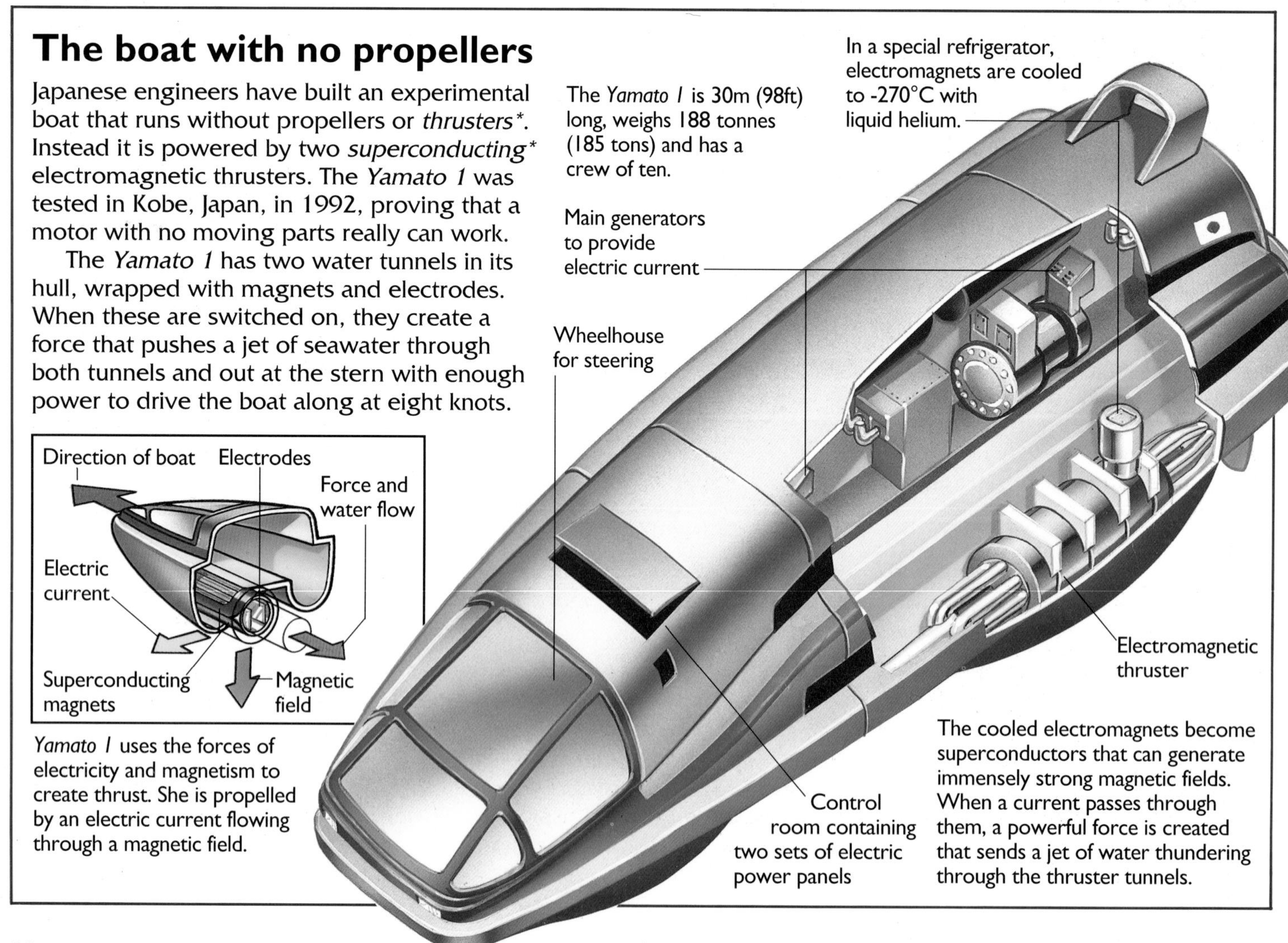

Yamato 1 uses the forces of electricity and magnetism to create thrust. She is propelled by an electric current flowing through a magnetic field.

Wave cutter

The knife-blade bows of fast catamaran ferries work so well that they may one day be used on cargo ships too. In the model below, the crew's quarters and the bridge are pushed up front, while as much deck space as possible is left free for freight. Up to 70 containers are stored out in the open, without hatches or covers. This saves weight and so makes the ship much faster.

Incat

This 40 knot wave-piercing freighter, designed by Incat, Sydney, Australia, is powered by four jet thrusters.

Flying boats

The most dramatic way to make boats faster is to lift them right out of the water altogether. One design that does this is the wing in ground-effect craft, or wingship.

The *Flarecraft L-325* rides smoothly on a cushion of air. Short stubby wings flying just above the surface of the water create a pocket of high air pressure (called ground effect) when they are moving at high speed. This will lift the 9.5m (31ft) craft into the air once it reaches 80km/h (50mph). But it cannot fly higher than 2m (6ft) above the waves, which is why it is registered with the US Coast Guard as a boat.

Flarecraft

This *Flarecraft L-325* is a five-seat water taxi, which cruises at 120km/h (75mph).

Glossary

Ballast. Heavy weights, often lead or tanks of water, packed into the deepest parts of the hull or keel to give a boat better balance. Ballast stops a boat from rolling over in heavy winds and waves.

Bow. The narrow front end of a boat, pointed to cut cleanly into the water.

Bridge. The place from which ships are steered. Usually one of the highest places above deck with a good view.

Bulkheads. Walls and watertight doors that run from side to side inside the hull and divide it into watertight compartments.

Buoy. A bright float, anchored near ports, used for navigation or mooring.

Coxswain. The person who steers a boat. Also called a helmsman.

Deck. The floors of a ship.

Dinghy. Any small boat powered by sail, oars or outboard motor.

Drag. The force created by the action of water against the hull and propeller of a ship which slows it down. Ships with long, narrow hulls and pointed ends usually suffer less drag than those with wide hulls and blunt ends.

Driveshaft. The shaft that transmits power from the engine to the propeller in a ship. Also called the propeller shaft.

Funnel. The chimney of a ship which releases smoke and exhaust gases.

Horsepower. A measurement of a boat's engine power, equivalent to 746 watts.

Heat exchanger. An attachment to a ship's engine to pipe cold seawater past the hot water that cools an engine. The seawater draws off heat, without coming into direct contact with the engine.

Hull. The part of a ship which sits in the water.

Hydrofoil. A boat with underwater "wings" designed to generate lift. As speed increases, the hull is raised out of the water, so reducing drag.

Keel. The lowest structure of a ship's hull, running lengthways, upon which the framework of the hull is built.

Knots. The speed of a ship in water is measured in knots, or nautical miles per hour. One knot is 1.85km (1.15 miles).

Lift. The upward force created by wings.

Port. Facing toward the bow of a ship, its left-hand side is known as the port side.

Propeller. A rotating device, with two or more curved blades, that provides thrust for moving a ship forward. A propeller is attached to a shaft (usually at the back of the boat) that is turned by the engine.

Radar. A method of finding the position and speed of a distant ship or other object, by transmitting radio waves which are reflected back to the sender.

Rudder. A large blade at the back of a ship behind the propeller, for steering.

Stabilizers. Fins projecting from the sides of the hull, to help keep a ship steady.

Starboard. Facing toward the bow of a ship, the right side is known as starboard.

Stern. The back end of a boat, usually rounded so water flows smoothly past.

Superconducting. Having no electrical resistance. In metals this occurs when they are cooled to very low temperatures.

Thrust. The force which drives boats forward, provided by the turning action of the propellers which throws a powerful surge of water backward.

Thrusters. Extra propellers in the hull of a ship for moving sideways.

Turbine engines. High-speed engines that work like the jets that power planes.

Upthrust. The force pushing up on a boat when it is floating in water.

Wheelhouse. An enclosed platform from which a ship is steered. Also called the pilothouse or bridge.

Winches. Winding wheels for raising and lowering heavy anchors, or for hauling ropes to raise sails or tie up to a dock.

Index

First published in 1996 by Usborne Publishing, 83-85 Saffron Hill, London EC1N 8RT, England.

UE. First published in America in March 1997. Printed in Italy.